Lust & Distrust

Lust & Distrust

Darlene Duncan

First Paperback Edition © 2022 Darlene Duncan
ISBN: 978-0-9723324-7-7

Published by Ocean Breeze Publishing

To Charlotte, the love of my life,
my biggest fan and with whom
all things are possible.

CHAPTER 1

I walked into My Place and took a deep breath of the wonderful smells. The aroma of fresh brewed coffee mingled with fresh baked pastries, and breads. The tinkling of the chimes over the door announced my entrance.

Harriet stuck her head out of the kitchen to see who had arrived. "Hi Laurel, I'll be out in a minute. I just need to finish up…"

"Go." I waved her back into the kitchen. "Finish whatever it is you're in the middle of, I'll get myself a cup of coffee."

The word coffee still hung in the air when the swinging door closed on her, as she returned to the kitchen and whatever delightful edible she was working on.

I hesitated for a moment on whether to grab a to go cup or one of the thick ceramic mugs for my coffee. Since I wasn't sure how long I was going to hang around I opted for the paper cup.

Sitting at my favorite table by the large window with a view of the beach across the street I sipped my coffee and waited.

As she came out of the kitchen wiping her flour covered hands on her apron, Harriet called out, "Hey chère." Her soft lilting New Orleans accent made everything sound sexy. "How're you doing today?"

"I haven't decided yet." I answered with a sigh.

Harriet laughed as she took the chair across from me. "Girl the day is almost gone, and you haven't decided…" She sounded exasperated and lightly slapped the tabletop. "You need to stop worrying and start enjoying life."

Smiling and shaking my head. "Harriet, how do you expect me to enjoy life when Natalie Kramer's killer is still running around loose?"

"Chère, there are all kinds of killers running around loose in this world, you can't let that keep you all tied up in knots."

Studying my coffee cup, I quietly said, "Yeah, well that may be, but I'm not a 'person of interest' in any other murders."

She leaned back in her chair. "Now we're getting to what the real problem is." She enunciated each word as if it were a complete sentence. "Detective Angela Murdoch." Leaning forward she continued, "You told me that she doesn't believe you killed that girl, so what's the problem?"

I brought my eyes up and looked at Harriet. "The problem is that she also told me she's not the only one investigating Natalie's murder and…"

Harriet looked at me. "And what?"

I sighed. "You're going to think I'm paranoid."

Harriet laughed. "Just because you're paranoid, doesn't mean there's not someone after you."

"Yeah, well, lately, I feel like someone's following me." I leaned forward. "For instance, on my way here I kept seeing the same car behind me but then it turned off two blocks away." I sat back in my chair. "Probably just someone headed home from work."

"Considering all the craziness you've been through lately – why don't you ask Murdoch to look into it. I remember when Alan was after me, having that feeling. He even bugged my apartment in one town."

"Right now, I'm not speaking to Murdoch."

"Why not?" Harriet waved her hand in the air as if to wipe away the question. "Never mind. How about Amber, have you forgiven her for lying to you about why she was in Coventry Beach?"

I took a long drink of coffee before responding. "I'm not sure about that one either." I paused. "I know she was just doing her job but still I have a problem with people who lie to me." I took a sip of my coffee. "And not only did she lie to me she tapped my phone, her and that Brian character."

Harriet stared out the window. There was still quite a bit of daylight left but it wouldn't be long before the sun would set, and the beach would be dark. It was still turtle nesting season and lighting restrictions were enforced. Talking out loud to herself Harriet said, "I wonder who they'll send to finish up that human trafficking case."

I laughed and said, "You haven't heard? I thought you knew everything that went on in this town."

She brought her gaze back to me and squinting her eyes demanded, "What do you know" she did a quick survey of the room to be certain we were alone "Larissa Carpenter?"

Harriet was one of the few people who knew my real name and I appreciated that she was careful not to use it where others could overhear. "It's just funny that you brought up

Amber because rumor has it that she's the one coming back to town to finish that human trafficking case." I stood up. "Aren't you ready to close this place? Let's go somewhere for dinner. Let someone wait on you for a change."

A big smile split Harriet's dark caramel colored face showing white teeth. "We're not going anywhere. Not after I spent the afternoon making something special for you."

She glanced at the timer she wore on her wrist. "It'll be out of the oven in about ten minutes." She pushed herself out of her chair. "You can set the table – for four."

"Four? Who are we dining with?"

"Never you mind that. Just get the table set." She headed back to the kitchen. "I'm going to check on dinner." Harriet paused at the kitchen door. "Before you set the table turn off the open sign, close the blinds, and lock the front door."

"Yes, ma'am."

CHAPTER 2

FBI Special Agent Amber Hoffner sat in her car in the parking lot of the Sheriff's sub-station in Coventry Beach.

Her mind replayed her last visit to the small beach town. A visit that ended with her killing the man who shot her.

She took a deep breath and entered the sub-station. The cadet at the front desk wasn't Cadet Donner. Amber watched the young man with his nose in a book. Before she reached the bullet-proof glass, he closed the book and looked up.

"What can I do for you?"

"FBI Special Agent Amber Hoffner, I'm here to see Detective Murdoch."

The young man smiled. "Yes ma'am. I'll let her know you're here."

Amber watched him as he used the phone to contact Murdoch. He had closed the book he'd been so engrossed in when she came in. It was a manual on police procedures.

He put down the phone, smiled at Amber and said, "She'll be right out, Special Agent Hoffner."

"Thank you."

Moments later, Murdoch opened the door leading back to the squad room and her office.

5

"Welcome back Special Agent Hoffner. It's good to see you again."

"It's good to see you too Detective Murdoch."

Their exchange was professional. Neither woman gave any evidence that they were anything more than colleagues. Their friendship had been forged in the danger they had faced together; however, they preferred that people operate on the belief that they were simply coworkers.

As they walked to Murdoch's office Amber looked around at the familiar surroundings. There were two desks, back-to-back in the middle of the room. Along the edges of the room were some bookshelves, a supply cabinet, a couple of small file cabinets, a large white board, and two printer / fax / copy machines. There were also two cots with their mattresses rolled up on top of the metal springs. To one side of the breakroom was Murdoch's office and to the other side was a conference / interrogation room.

Murdoch closed her office door and pulled the blinds on the large window. "Now that we're alone" she sat down in her desk chair "how are you doing?"

Amber pretended to not understand. "I'm not sure what you mean, detective?"

Murdoch tilted her chair back. "Oh it's, detective, is it?" She moved forward and rested her arms on the desk. "If you don't want to talk about Brian, excuse me, Special Agent Scott being transferred clear across the country or how the wounds from your last visit to Coventry Beach are healing, that's fine by me." Murdoch shrugged and before Amber could form a response, was on her feet. "Come on. We'll take my car. I'll bring you back for your car later."

Amber stood up. "Where are we going?"

Murdoch didn't answer but continued toward the front door of the station. At the door to the parking lot, she turned to the cadet at the reception desk. "You know how to reach me."

Cadet Wilson saluted her and went back to his studies.

On the sidewalk Amber stopped and demanded, "Where are we going?"

"Dinner."

CHAPTER 3

I saw Murdoch's car pull into the parking lot at My Place. *If Murdoch's the third person, who's the fourth?*

Then the passenger door opened and FBI Special Agent Amber Hoffner stepped into view. I took a deep breath and let it out slowly. I unlocked the front door, pushed it open, and hollered, "It's open. Lock it behind you."

I let the door close and headed for the kitchen. "So, you knew about Amber after all."

Harriet's face widened into a mischievous grin. "Never said I didn't."

Mentally reviewing our previous conversation, I realized she was right. She may have implied that she didn't know about Amber, but she didn't say she didn't know.

"Put that on the table." Harriet pointed at a cloth covered basket. "And take the butter dish with you. I'll be out in a minute."

The heat and the aroma of fresh baked biscuits wafted up from the basket as I carried it to the table.

Dinner was a delicious Shepherd's Pie and conversation was polite and pleasant. After dinner, I helped Harriet load the dishwasher and made sure Murdoch and Amber had to-go containers for their leftovers.

Stepping back into the kitchen I said, "What's for dessert?"

"You never mind, what's for dessert. You just go on out there and be sociable." She waved me out of the kitchen. "I'll be out shortly."

I turned to leave when she stopped me.

"Wait a minute." Wiping her hands on a towel she moved to a tea tray. It held a large teapot under a cozy and four teacups. Each teacup was under its own cozy, telling me Harriet had already warmed them.

She surveyed the arrangement and satisfied that it was complete said, "Take that tray with you."

Knowing better than to argue with her I picked up the tray and returned to the dining room.

The conversation between Murdoch and Amber stopped as soon as I came into the room. Refusing to be upset by this, I painted a smile on my face and said, "Harriet will be out with dessert in a moment. In the meantime, you can get started on your tea."

There were the appropriate murmurs of appreciation for Harriet's tea and queries about what was for dessert.

I held up my hands in surrender and said, "I have no idea what dessert is, so I'll be as surprised as you."

The crème brûlée was the best I had ever tasted. Afterward, as we all sipped our tea an awkward silence fell over the table. All the compliments to the chef had been delivered and it was as if no one could think of anything to say. Or maybe it was just everyone was afraid to say anything.

Finally, Harriet broke the silence. "Is this how it's going to be? Everybody afraid to talk about the big old white elephant in the room?" She looked around the table from one person to

9

the next. Shaking her head, she continued, "Everybody at this table knows that LC did not kill that girl, so why is there still this uneasiness between you three?"

A sudden thought occurred to me. "Is that why I keep feeling like I'm being followed? Because one of your agencies has decided to start tailing me everywhere I go?"

I knew Harriet was watching Murdoch and Amber for their reactions to my accusation, just as I was.

Murdoch's eyes instantly went to Amber and just as quickly Amber looked at Murdoch.

Then Murdoch turned to me. "It's not that anyone here" she emphasized the last word "thinks you were in any way involved in the murder of Natalie Kramer but..."

I pushed my chair back and stood up, knocking the chair over. "But what?" I looked back and forth between Amber and Murdoch. Their expressions spoke volumes. "You have got to be kidding me! Seriously, you two think I'm involved with the human trafficking."

Before anyone could say anything, I spun on my heel and ran from the building. Leaving the parking lot, I hit power mode and floored the gas pedal.

CHAPTER 4

Sitting at the table in stunned silence, Harriet looked at Amber and Murdoch. "Tell me she's wrong."

Murdoch leaned forward and holding Harriet's gaze said, "She's wrong. We" she indicated herself and Amber "don't think she's involved. At least I know I don't believe she's involved." She looked at Amber.

Shaking her head in disbelief that this issue was being blown so out of proportion by LC and Harriet, Amber said, "Bureaucracy moves slow on a good day. Added to that is the new supervising agent that was just assigned to our office. He's got more than just this one case and he has to get up to speed on all of them. Then he lets his opinion of each case be known by the agents working the case." She sighed. "I haven't even met the man yet. All I know is he was transferred in from the Chicago office."

"Harriet, until the FBI clears LC my office has to keep her as a suspect."

"Is she being followed? I know that feeling. It's very stressful."

Amber and Murdoch exchanged glances. Then they both turned to Harriet and started to speak at once.

"I think..."

11

"As far as I…"

"One at a time, ladies."

Murdoch indicated Amber should speak. "As far as I know, no one from the FBI is following LC." She tilted her head. "Although, I'm not sure they'd tell me if she was being followed."

Murdoch said, "I think I'd know if one of my department was following her. We don't have the kind of manpower to do that for any extended period."

"Larissa told me that she feels like she's being followed." Harriet looked from one to the other. "If it's not one of you, then who is it?"

The stunned looks on the faces before her at the mention of LC's real name, would have brought a smile to her face under other circumstances. "Yes, I know her real name. She trusted me enough to tell me." Harriet stood up. "However, I'm certain that you two found out some other way." She paused. "Maybe she's right to not trust you." She sighed. "I'm tired, ladies." She walked to the door and held it open. "Good night."

They rode back to Murdoch's office in silence. Sitting in the parking lot, Murdoch broke the silence. "You know, Harriet asked the right question. If it's not one of our agencies following her, who is it?"

Amber drew in a long, deep breath. "Maybe no one's following her and LC's just being paranoid."

"You're the one who's going to have to find the answers to that. My boss only still has her as a person of interest because your agency hasn't cleared her."

She sighed. "Speaking of bosses, I haven't met my new Supervising Agent, yet. Don't know much about him. I'm supposed to meet him tomorrow and get assigned a new partner."

CHAPTER 5

FBI Special Agent Amber Hoffner entered Central City's Regional FBI Headquarters the next morning. Shortly after she arrived at her desk, a deep, masculine voice behind her said, "Special Agent Hoffner?"

She spun her chair around as she stood up. "Yes, and you are?" Amber found herself staring at a man's chest. She tilted her head back a bit and raised her eyes to meet his.

"FBI Special Agent Thaddeus…"

Amber said, "…Joshua Robertson."

"You've done your research." He smiled and extended his hand. "Please, call me Josh."

Amber shook his hand. "You transferred in from the Mid-West with our new supervisor. What's he like?"

"Actually, I came in from Detroit. Michael was brought in from Chicago."

"So, you're on a first name basis with the new boss."

His smile faded. "Once a upon a time I was." He paused and Amber waited. "I was in Chicago for a while, then I got transferred to Detroit. I was there for a little over a year and now I'm here."

Amber watched his smile come back. "I like the warm weather." Not giving her time to ask any more questions, he continued, "I understand that you were originally in the Cyber Unit, why did you leave a cushy computer gig?"

"It wasn't my idea, at least, not a first. There was an individual we needed to get close to and I knew her from high school." She grinned. "Once I had a taste of field work, I decided to stay."

He raised an eyebrow. "In spite of getting shot, you opted for field work over an air-conditioned office where no one was going to be trying to kill you." Shaking his head, "If I had the level of computer skills necessary for the Cyber Unit, I would not be doing field work."

Amber shrugged. "Different strokes for different folks. How long has Supervising Agent Goldman been here?"

"A week." He laughed. "I think he misses the big city."

"What makes you say that?"

"Just a feeling."

Amber wanted to know more but got the impression that Josh wasn't interested in sharing information about Supervising Agent Goldman. "So, what's your feeling about this human trafficking ring?"

CHAPTER 6

FBI Supervising Agent Michael Goldman took a deep breath of the highly oxygenated air in the Heart of Palms Casino, as he surveyed the room. He was surprised that the casino was the equivalent of what he experienced in much larger cities. Central City wasn't the size of Chicago, so when he was transferred there, he feared he wasn't going to be able to find a place where he would be comfortable exercising his gambling addiction.

Though to Michael, gambling wasn't an addiction. It was a hobby. Some men fish, others bowl, or golf. Michael gambled. No big deal.

But it was a big deal. Gambling was illegal in Florida, and he was an FBI agent. Of course, that was part of the thrill. Not only did he risk losing money. Every time he entered an illegal casino, he risked his career.

Tonight, he headed for the poker tables and found an empty seat at a table of Seven Card Stud.

He directed his inquiry at the dealer, "May I?"

No one spoke but the dealer indicated he should be seated.

Normally, Michael brought only the amount of cash he was willing to lose. However, things weren't going well at home. He and his wife were fighting. She wasn't happy with moving to Florida and was threatening to take their son and move back to Chicago.

He won the first hand. However, from there things went downhill. Michael didn't know it, but he had a tell. A tell that was obvious to one of the players at the table and it wasn't long before his money was gone.

"I'll be back in a minute, gentlemen. I need to get some more chips." Michael went to the teller and used his credit card to get another $500.00 worth of chips.

It wasn't a good night for Michael. He drank too much and lost more than he could afford. As he was leaving the casino, he didn't notice that he dropped his wallet.

Rita Simmons scooped it up. Looking around, she noticed that one of the security guards saw her pick it up. She opened the wallet and called out, "Michael."

Seeing that she was headed toward the owner of the wallet, the security guard moved on to other things. When Rita had looked inside for his name, she saw his FBI ID.

Rita was a survivor, and she had a quick mind. Continuing toward the door she again called out, "Michael."

He turned around. "Yes? Do I know you?"

"No." She held out his wallet. "You dropped this."

He laughed. "Thanks. If there were any money left in it, I'd give you a reward." His words were slurred from too many Bourbons.

"That's okay." She looked concerned for him. "You look a little unsteady there. How about if you let me drive you home?"

"Home? Not my home. Explaining you to my wife would be…" He smiled and his face lit up, like a child at Christmas. "How about your place?"

Rita returned his smile. "Sounds good to me."

She put him in the passenger side of her car and then slid behind the wheel. "I just need to call my – roommate, to let her know I'm bringing home company." She reached across him, pulled the seatbelt toward her, and clicked it into place.

"Sure."

Rita was fairly certain he was passed out, but she was still careful in her choice of words. "Hey Donna. Yeah, I'm bringing home company. No, he'll only be with us long enough to sober up. I didn't want to let him drive drunk. See you in about ten minutes."

Thankfully, Rita and Donna's apartment was on the ground floor. Donna came out wearing a long robe to help her mother get Michael inside the apartment. It didn't take much for the two women to position him on his knees at the side of the bed, drop his pants, and leave his bare ass showing. Donna dropped her robe, revealing the black leather corset, fish net stockings, and high heels of a dominatrix. Then she grabbed a riding crop.

Rita was nowhere to be seen. She had taken up her position in the next room. Her job was to operate the video camera.

Donna's face would not be seen; however, Michael's face would be clearly visible.

Donna looked toward her mother's hiding place and asked, "Ready?"

Rita knocked on the wall, signaling that she was ready.

18

Donna brought the riding crop down on Michael's bare flesh. The pain brought Michael back to consciousness with a start.

He tried to stand up, but he got tangled in his pants and ended up on the floor with Donna atop him. Rita smiled as she calculated the riches this chance encounter would bring her.

Michael looked up at Donna with a smile. "How did you know I've…" he hiccupped "…I've been a bad boy? Huh?"

Donna helped Michael onto the bed, keeping her back to the camera. She took Michael's shoes and pants off and straddled him. Lying on top of him she moved in as if to kiss him, whispered something in his ear, and got off the bed.

Michael tried to stay awake while he waited for Donna to return but in a matter of minutes he passed out, again.

A few hours later, the sun shining on his face Michael woke. He tried to cover his eyes with his hands but found he was shackled to the metal headboard.

"What the…?"

Completely naked, his hands chained above him, and legs chained to the bed posts, Michael forgot about his hangover. "Where am I? Who the hell are you?"

Rita was standing at the foot of the bed, smiling. "I'm the woman who owns you, FBI Supervising Agent Michael P. Goldman." She could see his mind slowly realizing his situation.

Yes, he could scream for help and maybe a neighbor would hear him and call the police. But did he really want to be found by the police naked, chained to a bed. Definitely not.

"What do you want?"

Rita's smile broadened. "First, let me show you why you're going to do everything I say." She pressed the television remote.

Michael watched enough of the video from the previous night to know he didn't want to see any more of it. "Enough." Rita let it play for another ten seconds, just to show him that she was the one in control.

"What do you want?"

"For starters, there's a person I want to know everything about."

"You could have hired a Private Investigator."

"Yes, but they would have expected to be paid." She ran Donna's riding crop down his chest to his crotch. "*You* I don't have to pay, and *you* have access to things no PI has access to. Don't you?"

Michael glared at her. His desire to be dominated was a product of his drinking and he was sober.

"I asked you a question Michael and when I ask a question, I expect an answer." Not receiving an immediate response, she brought the riding crop down on his stomach. She smiled at his scream of pain.

"Okay. Yes, I have access to things no PI can use."

"That's better. And in case you have any ideas about having me arrested or killing me, know that this video file, photos of your driver's license, and photos of your FBI ID are all scheduled to be posted on the internet. The only thing stopping them from going live is me. Every day I have to re-schedule the posting." Rita picked up some photos she'd printed of the previous night's activities. She had trimmed one to fit in his wallet. It showed his face and the riding crop as it impacted his bare ass. While his facial expression was one of surprise, it could be interpreted as one of pleasure.

Leaning close to his face, she showed him the picture. "You will carry this in your wallet at all times. As a reminder. Whenever we meet, I'm going to ask to see this picture. Every time you don't have it, I post a picture. The wallet picture minus your face will be the first one I post."

Michael looked at her stone faced. It was a good thing he was chained because at that moment he would have gladly strangled the life out of Rita Simmons and the consequences be damned.

Rita smiled as she placed the photo in his wallet. "Now, I'm going to release your legs." She undid the shackles around his ankles. "Roll over."

Michael hesitated and Rita repeated her order. "Roll over."

Realizing he didn't have a lot of choice, he obeyed her. Michael bit down on the pillow to avoid crying out in pain as she delivered five powerful strokes of the riding crop to his backside. As she brought down the sixth stroke she said, "This one is for not obeying immediately. A reminder of who's in charge."

Rita placed an eight by ten glossy of the wallet photo on top of his clothes on the chair across the room, tossed the keys to his wrist shackles on the bed, and as she walked out the door said, "I'll be in touch, FBI Supervising Agent Goldman."

By the time he maneuvered the keys where he could use them to unlock his wrist shackles, the welts on his ass were quite painful. He tried to ignore them as he dressed. Pulling his pants on, especially his underwear, was agonizing.

That bitch, really put some muscle behind that riding crop. I've never had this much pain before.

He spotted the riding crop on the bed, where Rita had left it. Feelings of arousal began to move through him. He forced them down. He was going to be late for work and on top of that, he didn't have time to go home and change clothes.

Michael called a taxi, and then his wife. His call went to voice mail. He left her a message, blaming work for not coming home last night.

He looked at the background picture on his phone, expecting to see a picture of his son. It was a picture that always made him smile. Instead, he saw the picture Rita ordered him to always have with him.

"Bitch!"

While he waited for this ride, he returned the background picture on his phone to that of his son

CHAPTER 7

Rita and Donna met at their favorite restaurant for a late breakfast. Donna already had a table by the time her mother arrived.

"So how was our guest this morning?"

Rita smiled. "Obedient."

Donna returned her smile. "He doesn't seem to have a lot of money. Exactly, how are you planning on making use of him?"

Even though Donna was her daughter, Rita wasn't about to trust her with Michael's identity. She sipped the coffee that was waiting for her. "No, he doesn't have any money to speak of; however, he's going to help me acquire the money that is rightfully mine." She picked up a menu. "Let's order."

Looking over the top of her menu, Donna studied her mother, and decided she needed to find out who this man was.

Following their meal, while relaxing over coffee, Rita texted Michael. "Subject is Larissa Carpenter, widow of Rachel Simmons. Want everything you can find out about her. Slide under apartment door tonight. No later than 8:00 p.m."

Michael's emotions were in conflict when he read the text. Anger. Arousal. Curiosity. He plopped down in his office chair and was instantly reminded of why he would be standing at his desk for a day or two. He rose from the chair as if it had pushed him up.

His desk was adjustable, so he pressed the button and waited until it was the perfect height for him to work at, while standing. Logged into his computer he sent an order to a staff member to research Larissa Carpenter.

By that afternoon at 4:30 p.m. there was a file delivered to him. It contained everything about Larissa Carpenter, from birth to the present day.

His legs were getting tired, and he started to pull his desk chair over. The movement caused the fabric of his shorts to rub on one of the welts, reminding him why he was standing. Before leaving Rita's apartment he'd looked at his ass in the mirror. There were only two red welts on his buttocks. Three strokes in each of the two locations, was why the pain was so intense.

Rita had made sure to land her blows exactly where she wanted them for maximum affect. The welts would be gone in a few days, but it would take at least a week for the bruising to heal.

There was little doubt that it would be days before he would be able to undress in front of his wife. If she saw those welts, he'd have a lot of explaining to do.

Damn it! Our anniversary is in a week. I can only hope that I've healed by then.

He paced his office going through the file on Larissa. The early years he quickly skimmed. He slowed down and paid attention to the lottery winning and the death of her spouse, Rachel Simmons. Thinking ahead he sent a new order. He wanted the file on the death of Rachel Simmons, including the autopsy results.

On my desk before 6:30 p.m.

Rachel Simmons. Rita Simmons. Donna. I think I remember that name from last night. Rita's roommate's name was Donna. I think.

Larissa Carpenter was currently residing in Coventry Beach. The file included the Coventry Beach Sheriff's Office reports on the two crimes she had reported. His team was very thorough.

What the hell does Rita have in mind for this woman? He sighed. *Not my circus, not my monkeys.*

He scanned every page of the file onto a jump drive, while he waited for the file on Rachel Simmons death.

At 7:55 p.m. he was in the parking lot looking at Rita's apartment door. When his watch alarm went off at 7:59 p.m. he walked across the parking lot, slid the envelope containing both files under the apartment door, and walked back to his car.

CHAPTER 8

That night at midnight Michael's phone notified him of a text message. His wife mumbled something about getting texts in the middle of the night. Michael looked at the phone. "Sorry honey." He leaned over and kissed her on the forehead. "Go back to sleep. It's just work."

Meet me in the coffee shop on Fairview. Now.

He slipped on a pair of loose-fitting sweatpants, a t-shirt, placed his wallet in a shoe, put his cell phone in his pocket, and carried his shoes downstairs. He put his shoes on, leaning against the doorframe to the garage.

The ride home from work had been excruciating. Every bump and pothole in the road was a reminder of Rita. The thought of getting in the car filled him with dread but not as much dread as failing to obey her.

Traffic was light and ten minutes later he was at the coffee shop. Rita was checking her watch as he came through the door.

He walked to her table trying not to think about how much sitting down again was going to hurt.

"Sit down, Michael."

Having experienced what happens when he hesitated before, he knew better than to hesitate.

"What do you want?" He put his arms on the table and tried to keep some of his weight on them. "My wife doesn't like it when I get texts in the middle of the night. It makes her suspicious." He leaned forward. "And if she leaves me, half your leverage on me is gone."

Rita smiled. "Show me the picture."

Michael's jaw tightened. He had to take his arms off the table to get to his wallet. He forced himself not to grimace as he reached into his pocket.

Still smiling, Rita glanced at the picture, and said, "I have a job for you. Plant a bug in Larissa Carpenter's house. You can set up the receiver at this address." She pushed a piece of paper across the table.

Without looking at the paper, Michael said, "It's illegal to..."

Rita laughed. "Don't talk to me about legalities. Just get it done. Today."

"I have to sign out that kind of equipment and to sign it out requires a court order, which I don't have."

"Yes, well, I've taken care of that problem. That box on the seat next to you is the equipment you need. Just get it done today. I need to know her weakness." She smiled. "Everyone has one, don't they Michael?"

"Yes, I suppose they do." He paused. "Is that all?"

"No. I want you to stay out of casinos. Can't have you caught breaking the law and losing your position before I'm through with you."

Michael started to object but thought better of it.

"Anything else?"

"Just one other thing. I want her to stay a suspect in the death of Natalie Kramer. So do whatever you need to do to keep her from getting off the hook for that."

Michael remembered reading in the files he'd given Rita that the murder of Natalie Kramer was being attributed to one of the thugs who worked for the human trafficking ring the FBI was working on breaking up.

"Why do you care so much about this Larissa Carpenter?"

"She has something that is rightfully mine."

"What?"

"A fortune."

CHAPTER 9

Terri Snokes was having her third scotch when her phone rang.

"Hello," she slurred.

"Mr. Smith wants to see you, now." The call disconnected without giving her a chance to reply.

It was after nine o'clock at night.

Fuck 'em. They can wait until I finish my drink. She threw back the rest of the double scotch and ran the back of her hand across her mouth.

Sitting in her car in the driveway she thought about calling an Uber. She started to dial a number she had used before and then she remembered where she was going. She put her phone away.

Better I show up driving drunk than have an Uber driver drop me off.

She sighed and started the car, neglecting to fasten her seat belt.

As she drove to her meeting with Mr. Smith, Terri found she was constantly blinking to focus her eyesight.

The warehouse complex was poorly lit, and she slowed down to a crawl as she looked for her destination. Just ahead she spotted a large black SUV parked next to a building. She recognized the vehicle, and a mischievous grin turned her lips up. She applied what she thought was gentle pressure to the gas pedal. She swerved in time to only inflict a scrape down the length of the large black vehicle. The impact was still enough to deploy her airbag.

The noise of metal scraping on metal brought two men in black suits running from the building with guns in hand.

The first one to reach Terri's car yanked open the driver's door. He grabbed her arm and pulled her to her feet. Trying to avoid getting blood on himself, he leaned her against the car. Due to the blood running down her face he didn't recognize her at first.

Being drunk helped numb the pain caused by the airbag impacting her face. "Watch it big guy. That's no way to treat a lady."

Recognizing Terri, he grunted and then said, "Mr. Smith isn't going to be happy." He signaled his partner to deal with Terri's car.

Inside the building Terri raised her hands to shield her eyes from the light pointed at her and away from the man behind the desk.

A bit wobbly on her feet she staggered against her escort who roughly grabbed her arm to keep her from falling.

"Hey there, big guy, I already told you, that's no way to treat a lady."

Continuing to support her, he grunted and said, "She's drunk."

The cultured voice from behind the light said, "Obviously." He paused. "Put her in a chair before she falls down." As if he just noticed, he asked, "Why is she bleeding?"

As her escort put her in a chair he answered, "She ran into your car. Airbag got her."

The man behind the light inhaled audibly. "Ms. Snokes, what am I to do with you?"

The pain of her bloody nose and time were diminishing her alcohol induced bravado and fear was emerging, mixed with the pain of the airbag's damage to her face.

Terri licked her lips and swallowed hard. "I'm…I'm sorry Mr. Smith." She glanced up at the man mountain standing next to her chair and then back toward the voice behind the light. "I just…well, I mean, I was ordered to be here, and I'd been drinking." The words tumbled out of her like ants trying to escape a flood. "The caller hung up before I could tell them I shouldn't be driving and so I figured it was better to get here and I thought about calling an Uber but then I thought that wasn't a good idea. I only had two, maybe three, drinks." Her words were winding down. "I thought I could make it okay. I guess I was wrong."

Between three scotches, the last of which was a double, nothing to eat since breakfast, pain, and fear Terri's stomach was holding a rebellion. When she opened her mouth to speak again its contents erupted.

His voice dripping with disgust Mr. Smith ordered Terri's escort, "Let her sleep it off." He stood up. "Leave that mess. When she wakes up, have her clean it up, and then call me."

CHAPTER 10

When I left My Place, I started for home and then changed my mind. Sitting on the side of the road I called, Vera my favorite pet and house sitter. Vera would take care of the house and Tut for as long as needed.

An hour later I was at Greta's in Central City. I paid the cover charge and found my way to the bar. The same bartender was on duty as was the last time I visited.

"Seven-Up with a twist of lime."

It was still early, and the place wasn't crowded. There were a few couples sitting at tables in the darker recesses of the place with their heads together having intense conversations punctuated with long kisses.

The bartender delivered my drink. I handed him a ten and said, "Keep the change."

He smiled and said, "Thanks. Anything you need just ask for Ted. I'm your man."

I nodded in acknowledgement and moved to the game room in the back. One of the two pool tables was in use. Examining the rack of pool cues on the wall I chose one and racked the balls at the empty table. Just as I was about to break the woman at the other table spoke.

"Interested in a game?"

32

I straightened up and looked her over. Around five foot four, blonde hair, blue eyes wearing a black t-shirt with no logos or messages on it, and jeans. The soft Texas accent assured me that when she stepped from behind the pool table, she'd be wearing cowboy boots.

"Sure, why not. We'll flip for the break." I grabbed one of the quarters I'd lined up on the edge of the table and said, "Heads I break. Tails it's yours."

I lost the break. I also lost the game. Not that I cared. I was enjoying the view. It had been a very long time since I'd been with anyone and I was feeling a bit – I don't know what I was feeling but I ached to hold someone, anyone, in my arms, and to be held in return.

The exchange at My Place had assured me that Detective Angela Murdoch and I would not be getting any closer than we were. Cop and suspect, that was the limit of our relationship.

Rachel's passing was approaching the two-year mark and I needed physical contact. Just thinking about taking my pool playing friend to bed was causing my nipples to crinkle.

I won the second game and said, "Thanks for the games – you never told me your name."

"Elizabeth."

"Nice to meet you, Elizabeth. I'm LC."

As I twirled the pool cue in my hands I asked, "What brings you to Greta's?"

She racked her pool cue and turned to face me. "An Uber."

Without cracking a smile, I said, "So you're a comedienne." With more force than was necessary I pushed my pool cue into the wall rack. Cute wasn't cute tonight. Cute was annoying.

The two pool games had both proved challenging and more time had passed than I was aware of. The bar crowd had grown, and the volume of the music was higher. Though in the game room it wasn't so loud that you weren't able to carry on a conversation.

We stood less than a foot apart. A spicy lemon aroma wafted off Elizabeth and filled my nostrils. *Must be her soap or perfume. Either way it's making me hungry and not for food.*

A voice behind me said, "It is you."

I turned and saw the young woman I met the last time I visited Greta's. "Hi, Sara. Did things work out between you and your lady?"

"You could say that." She gave a small laugh. "When I walked back in here that night, she was already in someone else's arms." She shrugged. "So, I went home and threw her things out in the hallway."

She turned to my pool partner. "Hi, Beth. How's it going?"

"Okay." She looked from Sara to me and back at Sara. "I take it you two know each other."

Sara blushed lightly. "We've met."

I let my lips curve up slightly into an almost smile at the memory of our last meeting.

Beth smiled and turned to me. "Sorry for being such a smartass. It's just how I deal with strangers."

"Strangers and everyone else. Being a smartass just comes naturally for her." Sara laughed. "Don't let it bother you."

I suggested we find a table before they were all taken. As we left the game room the volume of the music hit me, and I took a deep breath. The air in the room was filled with perfumes and colognes, human sweat, beer, wine, and various alcohols, all battling for supremacy.

I ended up sitting between Beth and Sara. When a waiter stopped by to see if we needed anything, I said, "Tell Ted we need a fresh round here." The waiter hesitated. "He'll know what to give you."

I watched as our waiter conversed with Ted. When Ted looked our way, I smiled and waved. Moments later our drinks were delivered. I dropped a fifty on the tray and said, "Make sure that Ted gets his share."

The music was too loud to carry on a conversation. Fortunately, right after our drinks arrived the drag show started. The drag queens were in fine form.

It always amazes me to watch them dance in six-inch heels when I can't stand still on them without teetering on the edge of disaster.

When the show was over the music was still too loud for conversation. Looks were exchanged between Sara and Beth. During a lull between songs, I said, "Ladies, I think I'm going to call it a night."

I stood up and they rose too. They walked outside with me. Despite the humidity, the night air was refreshing after the recycled, scent laden air inside.

"It was nice to see you again Sara, and Beth thanks for the pool games."

"How long are you going to be in town?" Sara asked.

I shrugged. "Not sure. I don't have any plans for staying or leaving right now."

"Well, I have to work tomorrow, and I know Beth does too, but we could meet you somewhere for dinner."

"Okay. Where would you like to meet?"

Beth smiled. "That depends on what kind of food you're interested in."

I liked Beth's smile and thought she should do it more often. I handed each of them a card with my phone number on it. "I can usually find something I'm willing to eat at any restaurant. I'll leave it up to you two. Call me and let me know when and where."

CHAPTER 11

It was almost midnight when my phone rang. I looked at the screen. *Tammy Lopez. I wonder what she wants at this hour.*

"Hello Tammy. What can I do for you at the witching hour?"

"Huh? What? Oh my, I'm sorry. I didn't realize it was so late."

"No problem. I'm still up." I pulled my car over to the shoulder of the road. Tammy's sexy British accent deserved my full attention.

"Great. I'm headed to the coast tomorrow and wanted to know if you were interested in getting together for lunch."

"What are you doing right now?"

"Just leaving a party that broke up early. Why?" I could hear the smile in her voice.

I hesitated just a second. Then decided what the hell. "I'm in Central City. Would you like to meet somewhere for a drink and conversation?"

She didn't jump at the offer, but she didn't hesitate long either. "Sure. Where would you like to meet?"

"I'll leave that to you. You know the area better than I do. I'm staying at the Palm Garden Resort."

A short time later I walked into the bar at the Palm Garden Resort and chose a table where I could sit with my back to the wall and see all the comings and goings.

"Good evening. My name is Rita. What can I get for you?"

Rita. I flinched at the name. It was the name of the aunt that raised Rachel, disowned her when she came out, and then when Rachel died, accused me of killing her.

Placing a fifty-dollar bill on the table I said, "I'd like a pot of hot tea and a tray of finger sandwiches. The sandwiches will be on lightly toasted white bread, with cucumber, fresh spinach, tomato, and crispy bacon."

While it had taken me several months to learn that I could have whatever I wanted, if I was willing to pay for it, I tried my best not to act like a privileged asshole.

The young woman picked up the fifty. "It'll take about fifteen minutes, ma'am. Will there be anything else?"

I smiled. "A glass of room temperature water, no ice. Thank you."

Tammy walked, actually floated would be a better descriptor of how she entered the bar. It only took her seconds to spot me at the back table.

As she sat down, she asked, "How are things between you and Electra?"

I smiled. Somehow the fact that she remembered the name I gave the car I bought from her made me happy. "We're getting along fine."

Before either of us could speak our waitperson delivered my water.

I asked Tammy, "Is there something you'd like? I've ordered a pot of hot tea and some finger sandwiches."

Tammy looked at the young woman and said, "A double shot of Blanton's, neat."

Leaning back in my chair I studied my companion for a moment. Dark, short, spiky hair over expressive brown eyes.

"I don't remember you wearing glasses."

She smiled and gave a small shrug. "No, I wear contacts most of the time. I decided to give my eyes a rest tonight."

Tammy's drink arrived with my tea and sandwiches. "I do hope you didn't order that" she pointed at the tray "because of me."

I laughed. "No. I happen to like this as a late-night snack. But if you'd like some tea, I'm sure we can get another cup. For that matter, I'm willing to share the sandwiches."

"No thank you." She lifted her glass. "This will do very nicely."

In an effort to get a conversation started, I asked, "So how did you get into the car business?" Then took a bite of a sandwich and poured some tea.

Tammy studied me as if trying to decide how to or maybe if to answer my question. After several seconds, she asked, "Is that really what you want to talk about? My choice of careers?"

I finished chewing and washed the food down with some tea. "What would you prefer to talk about?"

Looking at me over her glass. "Why don't we discuss that in your room?"

I signaled Rita and per my request she found a room service cart, upon which I placed my tea and sandwich tray, along with another double of Blanton's for Tammy.

Trying not to let Rita's name prejudice me against her, I placed two twenties on the table.

The elevator ride to the tenth floor was conducted in silence. The faint aroma of Tammy's citrusy perfume mingled with the smell of tea, bacon, and bourbon. I found the combination appealing.

Inside the room I slipped the chain on the door and turned around to find Tammy wrapping herself around me. Her lips were pressed to mine, at first softly, and then with a more demanding force.

Her hands were roaming from my face down my sides to my waist. Then she slipped them under my shirt and unhooked my bra with experienced hands.

My body responded to her touch and my breathing became quite rapid. I tilted my head back, exposing my throat and she began a trail of kisses that was interrupted by my shirt.

In one smooth motion she pulled my shirt over my head and with it my bra. I don't know whether it was the chill air in the room, Tammy's amorous attentions, or a combination of the two that brought my nipples to full attention.

Soon we were on the bed, and I found out Tammy was more than a good salesperson.

Our love making was intense and though Tammy tried to prolong it, my climax came quickly.

"Wow! You were definitely ready."

Gasping for air, I smiled and played in her hair. "Don't worry about it. After being without for nearly two years, I'm surprised I didn't climax as soon as you touched me."

"Seriously? A looker like you?" She turned on her side to face me.

"Not in the mood for conversation." I pushed her onto her back and dusted off my love making talents.

Afterward, we lay on the bed naked and completely sated, as the ceiling fan quickly dried the light sheen of sweat from both of us. We made love at least two more times, before I fell asleep. I woke to the sound of running water. A smile pulled my lips up as I got out of the bed and headed to the bathroom.

Steam from the hot water filled the small room. I stepped into the open roman shower and pulled Tammy's soap slick body to mine. Before long I was weak kneed, and we were running out of hot water. I shut off the water and we each grabbed a towel.

Wrapped in the oversized bath towel, Tammy stood at the sink using her fingers to brush her hair. "How long are you in town for?"

"I'm supposed to meet some friends for dinner tonight, after that I'm not sure. I may head back right away or wait until morning." Wearing my own towel, I moved into the main room. "What are your plans?"

"Today's my day off. Originally, I was going to drive to the coast." Wearing only a damp towel, she walked to the bed where I was putting on my socks. Standing in front of me she dropped the towel and pushed me back onto the bed.

Laying on top of me and nibbling on my ear, she whispered, "How about we spend the day here?"

I rolled her off me. "Not today." I stood up and pulled my shirt on over my head. "Look last night, this morning, it was great…"

She propped herself up on her elbows. "I hear a but in there."

41

"But I'm not interested in a relationship." I paused. "Been there and done that. Don't have any interest in an encore."

Tammy rose from the bed and grabbed her clothes on the way to the bathroom.

Fully dressed, I was standing at the window looking out over the city. *Just another big city hotel room with a view of buildings and traffic.*

In the window I could see Tammy's reflection as she approached me. She wrapped her arms loosely around me. I turned to face her.

She looked me in the eyes. "Someone must have hurt you really bad." She sighed and then smiled. "But that's irrelevant, because I'm not looking for a relationship either."

A quick kiss and she pulled back from me. "Next time you're going to be over this way, give me a call. No strings just – fun."

As I watched her leave, I said, "I may just do that."

CHAPTER 12

Detective Angela Murdoch rang the doorbell at LC's house. It was mid-morning so she knew she wouldn't be waking her.

The door opened and a young woman Murdoch didn't know stood there holding Tut. "Yes, how can I help you?"

Murdoch hesitated. She hadn't been expecting a stranger to answer the door. "Is LC at home?"

"No." The young woman smiled. "I'm house and cat sitting for her. May I tell her you stopped by?"

"Do you know how long she'll be gone?" Murdoch sensed the young woman's reluctance at giving out such information and showed her badge. "I need to talk to her about a case we're working on. Do you know where I can find her?"

"Not really. I think she went to Central City, but she didn't give a specific return date. Sorry."

Murdoch hid her concern with a smile. "No worries. Thanks for your time."

At My Place, Murdoch walked past the customers in the dining room and the counter, straight into the kitchen. Harriet was just pulling a large tray of pastries from the oven.

"Where is she?"

Harriet knew who Murdoch was talking about but pretended not to know. "Where is who, detective?" She also wasn't

43

aware that LC had gone anywhere. Though after the previous evening, Harriet wasn't surprised that LC would take a break from Coventry Beach.

In a demanding voice loud enough to be heard outside the kitchen, "Larissa Carpenter. Where is she?"

Harriet considered Murdoch a friend. After all Murdoch had pulled her out of the house where her ex-fiancé turned stalker held her captive. However, she also knew that without LC's help, Murdoch wouldn't have been able to find her before she was dead. LC hired the search team; therefore, in Harriet's eyes, she ranked above Murdoch.

Harriet stopped removing the pastries from the tray she had placed on the stainless-steel table, narrowed her eyes, and walked to stand in front of Murdoch. "Even if I knew where she was, I wouldn't tell you." She paused and took a step back from her adversary. "Unless of course you have an arrest warrant. Do you have an arrest warrant, detective?"

Murdoch's jaw tightened and she forced her hands to not become fists. Without a word she spun on a heel and marched out of the building.

Harriet held the swinging kitchen door open and watched Murdoch get in her car. A quick glance around the dining area assured her that her customers, probably hadn't heard the exchange between herself and the detective.

CHAPTER 13

After Tammy left, I decided to head home. I couldn't think of a reason to stay another minute in Central City.

When I arrived home, I paid Vera a bonus for the short notice, saw her off, and headed for a shower, and clean clothes.

I really need to keep an overnight bag in the car.

As I was drying off, Tut wandered into the shower and rubbed up against my legs. "Yes, I love you too. Just sometimes I need more than you can give me, my furry little friend."

With Tut draped around my neck, halfway down the stairs, the doorbell rang. Looking through the peephole I saw Murdoch.

Standing in the doorway, I said, "Good afternoon, detective. What can I do for you?"

"You could invite me in."

"I could, but I don't see why I should."

Murdoch drew in a long breath and looked away and then brought her eyes back to me. "Please. I'd like to talk to you."

After a brief hesitation, I stepped aside and gestured her in, leaving her to close the front door.

On my way to the kitchen, I deposited Tut on the back of my recliner, rubbed his ears, and gave him a quick kiss on top of his head.

In the kitchen, I kept my back to Murdoch, as I got down a coffee filter, the coffee, and began preparing a pot of coffee. "Do I need to have my lawyer present for this talk?"

"No. But I would prefer to talk to your face, not the back of your head."

I wasn't ready to look at her yet, so I finished my prep work and started the pot brewing before turning around. I silently held her gaze, as if we were in a staring contest.

I remembered an old adage, whoever speaks first, loses and I had no intention of losing.

"I just wanted you to know that I don't think you're involved in the human trafficking ring. Neither does Amber. And neither of us thinks you were in any way involved in the death of Natalie Kramer." She paused.

I said nothing and continued to stare at her.

"Damn it, LC! I can't control the speed with which the FBI bureaucracy moves." She ran her hands through her short hair, making it stand on end. For some unknown reason, I found this mannerism amusing, and I almost smiled. Almost.

"Since we believe that Natalie Kramer's murder is somehow tied to the human trafficking gang, the FBI is in charge. This new supervising agent has to review the case file and once he has, I'm certain he'll see that there's no evidence that you're in any way connected to any of it."

Ignoring everything she said, I turned to get coffee mugs down. "So where is FBI Special Agent Hoffner, too chicken to come here with you?"

"What? No! She's meeting with an informant."

I spun around and unable to control the concern in my voice said, "You let her go alone?"

"No, I didn't let her go alone. She has another agent with her." Murdoch smiled. "You do care."

"Care?" I harumphed and turned back to the coffee pot. "Care about a sneaky liar who tapped into my phone, as if I were a criminal? I don't think so."

I picked up the glass carafe to pour the coffee into a thermos when I felt Murdoch close behind me. A shudder of delight ran through my body as her scent found its way to my nose and I felt the heat from her body on my back.

God, what does that woman wear that makes her smell like a crisp, sunny day on the beach?

"If you don't care, why were you concerned about her meeting an informant alone?" Her voice was soft and teasing.

"Unless you want me to spill this coffee, you need to give me some room." Even though my heart was racing, I kept my voice steady and emotionless. She stepped back and the smell of fresh brewed coffee helped clear my head.

I've got to stop this fantasizing about her. She's a cop and I'm a suspect, whether she admits it or not. I can't be with a woman who doesn't trust me and more importantly, a woman I don't trust. She's not telling me everything she knows.

I poured two cups of coffee and put the remainder in the thermos. Without turning to look at Murdoch, I headed to the back deck. "The cup on the counter is for you."

Standing at the far end of the unscreened portion of the deck I closed my eyes and listened to the sounds of the sea.

The surf, the wind, the gulls. I took a deep breath of the salty air and turned to face Murdoch.

She was just coming out of the screened in area.

"I have something to say, and I need you to let me say it."

"Okay."

"Without interruption."

Murdoch nodded her agreement.

"I thought, hoped, that we could at the very least be friends, but I've come to realize I can't be friends with someone who doesn't trust me and whom I don't trust." I held Murdoch's gaze, looking into those grey eyes, wondering how they could be so cold looking and yet so warm at the same time. "Going forward I believe our relationship should be strictly professional. Cop and suspect." I paused. "And the same goes for your colleague, FBI Special Agent Amber Hoffner."

Murdoch looked away and set her coffee cup on the nearby table. She straightened her shoulders, brought her eyes back to me, and with that closed poker face of hers said, "I wasn't it aware it was anything else, Ms. Carpenter."

Without another word she turned and took the path to the front of the house.

A few hours later I got a text from Sara.

"Dinner at Maggie's on Hibiscus Avenue? 6:30?"

Crap. I forgot I was supposed to meet her and Beth for dinner. Too bad. Maggie's has great food.

An idea occurred to me, and I texted back. "Sure. Love Maggie's."

A quick phone call and everything was set. Though I wouldn't be there, I was certain the two ladies would have a good time.

CHAPTER 14

The next morning right after rush hour, LC headed to Kellyville. With people trying to get to work or school off the roads, the tourist traffic was all she had to deal with.

A small town on the outskirts of Central City, Kellyville was the closest place to get the piece of equipment that she wanted – a bug detector.

She spent time thinking about what Harriet had said about how Alan had bugged her apartment at one time. While she knew that there wasn't any crazy ex-lover after her, she still had the feeling that someone was following her.

Like Harriet said, just because you're paranoid doesn't mean that there isn't someone after you.

Stan's Spy Shop had a small parking lot to match the small building that housed a multitude of privacy busting and privacy maintaining equipment.

She stopped just inside the door to look the place over. To her right was a Gilly suit on a hanger, next to that were wire shelves displaying a variety of gadgets, ahead of her was a glass counter. Inside the glass counter there was an assortment of knives and martial arts weapons. On the other side of the room was another glass case containing a variety of recording and listening devices. On the wall behind that glass case were bug detectors and everyday items that contained cameras.

The man at the desk behind the glass case in front of LC stood up. "Good morning. How may I help you?"

LC walked toward him. "I need a bug detector and I want to put some security cameras in my house."

"Okay." He stepped over behind the other glass case and pulled a small plastic device down. "This will find any device that emits a radio frequency." He turned it on and pointed it at LC's waist, where the holster holding her cell phone hung. The device began to beep. As he moved it back across the glass case, the beeping became softer until it stopped.

"Excellent." LC chose some devices containing cameras that would easily fit in with her décor. In less than thirty minutes she had chosen all her purchases and paid for them, with cash. "Thank you, Dan."

He seemed surprised that she knew his name. She smiled and said, "I like to know who I'm doing business with." On her way to the door, she stopped and turned around. "If I have any trouble getting all this connected, can I call you for assistance?"

"Sure. By the way, I know a good private investigator." He smiled. "If you think you're being followed, he can confirm or disprove that theory."

LC walked a few steps back toward Dan. "I didn't mention anything about being followed. What makes you think I might be concerned about that?"

"I've been in this business a long time. If you're being bugged, odds are you're also being followed."

LC considered the logic of the statement and then said, "Yes, that sounds like something I would be interested in." She pulled a business card from her wallet. "Here's my email address and phone number. Email your PI's information to me." She paused. "And yes, I'll be sure to tell him who referred me to him."

Once she was back out on the highway, LC set the cruise control at an appropriate speed. That way watching her speed was one less thing to which she had to pay attention.

The garage door was down by the time she stepped into the house. Her first mission was to find the listening device that her instinct told her was there.

She turned her cell phone off and then went back into the garage to the circuit breaker box. She flipped the master breaker off.

As she stepped back into the house, the silence was noticeable. None of the electronics were running. The refrigerator, the router for the internet, the televisions, there was no hum of electricity anywhere.

Standing at the foot of the stairs facing the garage door, LC was halfway between the living room and the breakfast nook. She turned to her left and walked the perimeter of the room, then she traveled a Z pattern across the room. Nothing.

She returned to her starting point and repeated the process for the kitchen and breakfast nook area. As soon as she turned to her right, the detector emitted a faint beep. LC moved into the kitchen and the beep all but disappeared. Walking toward the breakfast nook, the beeps increased in volume and frequency. Moving around the table the beeps slowed and the volume dropped. LC moved back toward the

51

corner, past the table, again the beeps slowed. She stepped back and at the north end of the sliding glass door she stopped. The beep was a steady tone.

LC ran the detector down to the floor and then back up toward the ceiling. Then she saw the almost invisible device. It was attached to the glass, in the top corner of the north half of the sliding glass doors.

She moved through the rest of the house without a beep, turned off the device, and turned her electricity back on.

As soon as her router let her back on the internet, LC began her research. The device was called The Fly. It picked up the vibrations the human voice created in the glass. There weren't a lot of details about the device. However, there were hints that a black-market version could be purchased by those with sufficient money.

Damn it! That means I could be bugged by anyone from the FBI to some civilian jackass.

Her new friend Dan told her that if she found a bug, she could render it virtually useless with white noise. LC downloaded a white noise app and began running it. She ran it for twenty minutes and then turned it off.

CHAPTER 15

Terri Snokes woke with a backache. The cot in the office at Mr. Smith's warehouse wasn't quite what she was used to sleeping on. She slowly moved to a sitting position on the edge of the thin mattress.

The only light in the room was coming in through a large window that looked out on the warehouse floor. It was sufficient for Terri to tell where she was without causing too much pain to her hangover.

It took her a few minutes to figure out why her face hurt as much as her head. Then like a movie on fast forward the events of her arrival at Mr. Smith's warehouse played in her mind.

She groaned. *Shit! This is not good.*

The door to the office opened and one of Mr. Smith's men was standing in the doorway. In a voice that seemed out of place in a man so large he said, "There's a mop and bucket out here waiting for you."

He turned and walked away, leaving the door open. Without his bulk blocking the doorway, light spilled into the room and Terri closed her eyes. A few deep breaths and she got to her feet. Her mouth tasted terrible and what she wanted, at that moment, more than anything in the world was a drink.

Instead, she asked the man mountain, "Can I get some water?"

With no change of expression, he tossed her a bottle of water before moving away from her to the far side of the room. Terri drained the bottle, found a recycle bin to put the empty bottle in, and began mopping up her mess.

She could tell it was still dark outside. A quick squeeze of the electronic exercise tracker on her wrist told her it was just before sunrise.

After she finished her mopping, she took the mop and bucket to a large sink against the wall and rinsed everything thoroughly.

She set the cleaning equipment on the floor next to the sink and headed for where the man mountain was sitting.

"When's Mr. Smith coming back?" She could see the earbuds in the man's ears, still she had no doubt he could hear her.

Standing in front of him she repeated her question. *Even if the asshole can't hear me, he can read lips.*

Rather than verbally answer her, he pointed to a chair several feet away, indicating she should sit down.

Terri narrowed her eyes and pursed her lips. Her hands curled into fists. She watched the man mountain's eyes move from her hands to her face and he smiled.

"Shit!!" She stomped over to the chair indicated and sat down.

The man mountain just sat there listening to whatever was coming through his ear buds. After what seemed like hours to Terri, he sat up, and began talking.

Must've gotten a call. Maybe Mr. Smith is coming or better still he says I can go.

The call was over, man mountain stood up, and walked to Terri. "You can go now. Be back here tonight at nine-thirty – sober."

Terri jumped up out of her chair and had to grab the back of it to steady herself. She needed food and coffee. As she walked across the warehouse to the door, she heard, "Remember sober."

CHAPTER 16

Murdoch was sitting at her desk fuming about her meeting with Larissa Carpenter when Special Agent Amber Hoffman appeared in her doorway.

"Wow! You look pissed at the world."

"Whatever." Murdoch stood up and turned her eyes to the tall handsome man with Amber. "Who's your friend?"

And I use the word friend loosely. Amber needs to watch out for this guy. He's got that same easy charm and big smile that Mike had.

She narrowed her eyes studying him.

And Mike nearly cost me everything.

"FBI Special Agent Thaddeus Joshua Robertson meet Detective Angela Murdoch."

He extended his hand with a smile. His full lips opened, showing straight white teeth. "Nice to meet you. Just call me Josh."

Both Amber and Josh noted the slight hesitation before Angela took his hand. "Nice to meet you too, Special Agent Robertson."

Eager to change the subject, Amber asked, "How did your meeting with LC go?"

"Ms. Carpenter is a person of interest in both of our cases. Let's leave it at that." She held Amber's gaze, almost daring her to pursue the issue.

For several heartbeats no one spoke. Then Special Agent Robertson said, "I think I'll get a cup of coffee. Can I bring either of you something?"

With their eyes still locked on each other, both women responded in stereo, "No."

Special Agent Robertson closed the door behind him.

"Ms. Carpenter? Really?"

"Her idea not mine." Keeping all emotion from her voice Murdoch sat down and continued, "Can we get back to business?" Nodding toward the door she asked, "Where did he come from?"

"Josh?" She sat down in the chair opposite Murdoch. "He's just who was assigned to work with me. Can't say I've had time to get to know him very well. He's alright, I guess."

Tilting her head, she gave Murdoch a questioning look. "Why don't you like him?"

"Who said I didn't like him?"

"You did." She sat up straight and leaned toward Murdoch. "The hesitance at shaking his hand. Calling him Special Agent Robertson, instead of Josh."

Murdoch rolled her head around from one shoulder to the other. "Just be careful of him. There's something about him I don't trust."

Amber had researched Murdoch's past. She wanted to know who she was working with, and she had learned about Mike Cornwall. Murdoch's former partner. A dirty cop who tried to frame Murdoch for his misdeeds.

In a quiet voice she said, "He's not Mike."

Murdoch processed the statement quickly. *She's done her research on me.* "Whatever. Can we get back to work? What did your informant have to say?"

Realizing that she wasn't going to sway Murdoch's opinion of Josh, Amber took a deep breath, sank back into the chair, and said, "Not much. He did give us an address of a warehouse that Mr. Smith likes to work out of. Josh and I are going to stake it out tonight and see what we can learn."

Murdoch sat down, glanced at a paper on her desk. "That wouldn't happen to be at 25698 Woodruff Road, would it?"

Amber leaned forward again and asked, "How did you get that address?"

Smiling Murdoch said, "I don't think I'm going to reveal my source, right now." She paused. "My guess is that Mr. Smith has a guy working for him by the name of James Thomas Rudzik, commonly referred to as JT."

Shaking her head Amber said, "I don't know why I should be surprised that you have better information than I can get. The benefits of being a local."

Before Murdoch could comment, Special Agent Robertson tapped on the door and then opened it. Amber stood up.

"How about if we all get something to eat? That place you recommended under the bridge was good. Do you like seafood, Josh?"

A smile split his face, and his eyes lit up. "Yes, I do."

"Excellent. On your feet Murdoch. This will be a working dinner to discuss the case."

Murdoch hesitated.

"Come on, detective. I know you can't resist hush puppies from there and the FBI is buying."

CHAPTER 17

Mr. Smith's warehouse was on the river that separated Coventry Beach from the mainland. It was part of a complex that included a small marina.

Amber parked the black SUV out of sight, half-way between the warehouse, and the river. After they grabbed their surveillance equipment, she turned on the signal booster, checked its power supply, and locked the vehicle.

"Let's go."

Each of them carried a backpack and a cooler. If anyone saw them, nothing would seem out of the ordinary. Just a couple of people headed for their boat with some supplies.

Standing on the dock looking at their living quarters for the night, Josh groaned.

The forty-foot classic sailboat was beautiful. The white hull was accented with teak trim, and the white boom tent covered most of the dark blue sail pack.

Amber looked at him. "What's the matter?"

"There are two reasons I joined the Air Force instead of Navy."

Amber smiled as she climbed aboard. "Yeah, what were they?"

"I don't like small spaces and I get motion sickness." He stepped onto the deck and clenched his teeth in preparation for the nausea he knew would soon arrive.

"Sorry but this was the best line of sight for our target."

They ducked under the boom and entered the cabin to set up their cameras. Once the still camera and the video camera were setup, Amber said, "The only thing left is to attach The Fly to the window."

She pretended to search for a coin. "Do you want to flip for it?"

Amber hadn't finished her question before Josh said, "No. I'll do it."

Amber laughed. "Fine."

As soon as it was full dark, Josh moved to the dock, and hit the light sensor on the parking lot light with a blast from his flashlight. Having been fooled into thinking it was daylight, the light went out, and he ran across the open space to the building. He was beside the warehouse before the light came back on.

A quick look through the window just past the entrance, showed an empty warehouse. He quickly attached the listening device, known as The Fly, to the upper right corner of the window. The Fly would pick up any audio inside the building by the vibrations of the glass, transmit it to the signal booster in the SUV, from there it would be routed to the recorder set up on the boat.

Not wanting to draw attention to the light going out again, Josh took the long way around to get back to the dock. Besides that, he wasn't in a great hurry to return to the boat's cabin.

Amber met him at the entrance to the cabin. She handed him a set of binoculars. "Why don't you stay out here in the cockpit? I've heard that if you're in the open the nausea isn't so bad. Just keep yourself out of sight."

Josh settled into the cockpit only lifting his head occasionally to look around.

The sound of a car drew his attention. A large black SUV like theirs pulled up close to the warehouse entrance. He could only see the driver's side of the vehicle. He heard the click of the still camera as Amber took multiple pictures of the driver, who got out and walked around to the other side.

James Thomas Rudzik, alias JT stood on the passenger side by the back door. Mr. Smith got out, took a quick look around and then moved to the warehouse door. Standing at the door punching in the code to unlock the building all Amber could see was the back of the man's head.

Damn it! Turn around. I want to see your face.

As if he'd heard her, Mr. Smith turned back to face the SUV. Amber shot half a dozen pictures of Mr. Smith.

"Get that damn bird off my car." Mr. Smith yelled at JT.

JT looked at the roof of the SUV and saw the owl that had startled his boss.

Mr. Smith entered the building and JT shooed the owl off the SUV. It flew up to the top of a light pole and hooted.

"I wonder if they're expecting company tonight." The words were barely out of Amber's mouth when another car pulled up and parked next to the SUV.

Amber turned the video camera back on and used the still camera for a series of shots of the woman before she entered the building.

A short time later, a quiet voice from the dock said, "Permission to come aboard."

Amber stuck her head out of the cabin. "Permission granted."

Murdoch stepped past Josh and entered the cabin. She surveyed the variety of surveillance equipment as she handed Amber a small plastic shopping bag. "Here you go. Hope these help."

"I'm sure they will. Josh."

Unfolding himself from the cockpit Josh entered the cabin as he freed one ear from the ear buds that allowed him to hear what was going on inside the warehouse. "Yes."

"Read the instructions." She passed the bag to him. "Put them on the right way and your motion sickness will stop." She shrugged. "They work better if you put them on before you start feeling symptoms. They'll just take a little longer to kick in since you're already not feeling well."

Josh looked from Murdoch to Amber and back to Murdoch. "Thank you."

Ignoring his presence Murdoch picked up a pair of binoculars and looking at the warehouse asked, "Who's the party for?"

"I wish I knew. The SUV pulled up. Two men went inside. I got good pics of both, thanks to an owl."

Murdoch looked at her. "An owl?"

"Yeah, never mind. You had to be there." She pressed the button on the printer and out came first a picture of JT.

"That looks like the man mountain I was told about."

The picture of the second man came off the printer.

"Can't say I know this one." She looked from the photo to Amber. "You have any idea who he is?"

Amber shook her head.

The printer spit out a third photo and Murdoch stared at it for several seconds. "This is Terri Snokes. She's head volunteer of the turtle patrol." She looked from Amber to the photo to the warehouse. "What the hell is she doing here?"

Amber switched the recording device to speaker, so they could all hear what was going on inside the warehouse.

"Apology accepted. Now we need to get down to business, Ms. Snokes."

"Yes sir."

"I know that one or more of my crew is involved in these turtle nest robberies and most likely, the death of that young woman. This is bringing unwanted attention to my business." He paused. "I want to know who they are, Ms. Snokes."

"Mr. Smith, I…"

He interrupted her. "Before you tell me a lie, know that I'm quite certain you know the names of these imbeciles. I have my suspicions. I simply need – confirmation."

Murdoch knew the speech pattern and inflections in the man's voice placed his point of origin somewhere in Europe. His total lack of accent marked him as a man who worked hard at hiding his origins while showing off his education.

"I only helped them because they told me you wanted the eggs, Mr. Smith."

Murdoch could almost see the dismissive wave of the hand as Smith continued, "Yes, I understand. Just give me the names."

Fear dripped from every word out of Terri Snokes' mouth. "Sailor and Curly, are all I know them by."

"Thank you, Ms. Snokes." He paused. "Now, about the job I gave you, have you planted the evidence implicating Ms. Carpenter?"

Terri's voice shook as she answered. "No, sir. I haven't been able to get into her house. All the passwords have been changed for everything."

Smith's sigh of disappointment was audible. "Don't worry about it, Ms. Snokes. I'll handle the situation. And you don't need to worry about Sailor or Curly bothering you again. I'll deal with their discipline personally."

"Yes, sir. Whatever you say."

"Stay here for as long as you need to calm yourself. We'll be in touch."

Mr. Smith's companion opened the warehouse door, and the two men got into the SUV and drove away.

Murdoch waited until she was sure the SUV was gone. "We need to go in there and get her, while she's feeling vulnerable and scared."

"I'm not sure that's the best idea."

"I am. I know this woman, if we wait until she has time to get over this meeting, we'll have a much harder time getting her to cooperate."

Murdoch moved out of the cabin and off the boat before Amber could say anything more.

"Come on Josh." The two FBI agents were right behind Murdoch as she went through the warehouse door, guns drawn.

Terri jumped and sat the whiskey bottle down on the table. Murdoch holstered her gun. "Take a look around," she directed Amber and Josh.

The look on Terri's face was a mixture of guilt, fear, and relief. Murdoch knew that Terri was going to help them.

"Terri, what are you doing working with these people? Your friend that just left…"

"He's not my friend," she screamed.

In a dark corner a few feet away, Josh called out. "Guys, we need to get out of here. This place is rigged to blow."

Murdoch grabbed Terri by the arm and headed for the door. Outside and halfway to the boat, the four of them were knocked to the ground by the explosion.

Lying on the pavement next to Terri, Murdoch looked at her and said, "Yeah, you're right he's not your friend. He just tried to kill you."

CHAPTER 18

It was after midnight by the time Murdoch and Amber walked into the interrogation room where Terri was waiting for them.

Murdoch glanced up at the camera in the corner, verifying that it was operating. Then she brought her attention to Terri.

"You've been read your Miranda Rights, haven't you?"

Terri nodded her head.

"I need you to affirm the answer verbally, Terri."

"Yes, you gave me my rights and one of the deputies recited them again after I arrived here."

Murdoch sat down next to Amber, who had a folder open on the table in front of her.

Amber placed a picture of Mr. Smith in front of Terri. "Tell us about this man."

Terri stared at the picture for several seconds before bringing her gaze up to Murdoch. "He's a black hearted bastard! What else do you want to know?"

Amber asked, "Why did he try to kill you tonight?"

Terri's eyes darted between the two women. "I don't know." She shrugged. "Maybe he decided he doesn't need my help anymore."

Murdoch leaned forward. "Exactly what kind of help were you giving him?"

Terri squirmed in her chair but said nothing.

"How much was it worth to you to send over seventeen girls to a life of slavery? Huh, Terri? How much?"

Her arms on the table Terri leaned toward Murdoch. "Not a penny. I never got a penny. It was just…" She sat back and fell silent.

"So, he had something on you. What was so terrible that you were willing to help this sick bastard?"

Terri hung her head, pulled in a deep breath, sat up straight in her chair, and said, "I hit someone with my car. They died. He found out and threatened to turn me in if I didn't help him."

Once she started talking Terri, gave them the whole sordid story.

"…By the time I realized he was selling young girls and women, it was too late. I was in so deep; I couldn't see a way out."

"What about Natalie Kramer and the turtle eggs?"

Silent tears ran down Terri's face. "I didn't know they were going to kill her. I thought they'd just add her to the ones being collected for transport."

She looked at Murdoch. "I'm sorry. I just couldn't figure out how to…"

"You just couldn't figure out how to get out, stay out of jail, and not get killed. In other words, all those girls and women, lost everything because you're a coward." Pushing her chair back Murdoch got to her feet and slammed the door behind her.

Later, Amber came into Murdoch's office. "She's writing it all down."

"Yeah." Murdoch's feet were resting on an open drawer. Her chair was tilted back as she repeatedly, tossed an exercise ball in the air and caught it. "What did she say about the evidence she was supposed to plant?"

"It's the gun that was used to kill Natalie Kramer." Amber sighed. "I've sent Josh along with a forensics team to her house to retrieve it."

Murdoch put her feet on the floor and turned her chair to face Amber. "I'm more concerned about what Smith has in mind next. He said he would 'handle the situation'. I doubt that means anything good for LC."

"Yeah, but whatever it is we have the recording of him saying he wanted LC framed."

Amber watched Murdoch for a few moments. "You do know Terri Snokes isn't going to do any jail time, don't you?"

Murdoch squeezed the exercise ball in her hand. "Not happy about it but not surprised." An evil smile lit up her face. "Just do me a favor."

"Sure, if I can."

"Make sure she ends up somewhere landlocked, either a desert location or in the mountains. Preferably a desert."

Amber smiled. "I'll see what I can do." She paused. "After you left, she said that there's one more group of women that haven't been shipped out yet."

Murdoch's feet hit the floor and she leaned forward. "I'm all ears."

CHAPTER 19

Murdoch surveyed the dining area of My Place as she held
the door for a couple on their way out. She had no desire to
run into LC.

"Good morning, detective."

"That remains to be seen." Murdoch smiled. "I see business
is going well."

Though Harriet was smiling, it wasn't the warm smile that
she gave to friends. It was a polite smile. The one she used
on customers. Harriet looked around the dining area, where
more than half the tables were occupied. "Yes. Things have
picked up. What can I get for you?"

"Coffee, black, and two cake donuts."

"To go?"

"No, for here. Special Agent Hoffner and her partner will be
here soon." Murdoch studied the menu board. "What does
Amber usually order?"

"Never can guess with that one. Sometimes it's the Two
Ladies. Other times she gets coffee and donuts, like you."

"Well, when she gets here, I guess she'll just have to order
her own stuff."

Murdoch paid Harriet and took her donuts and coffee to the
far table by the window. It was her favorite table because it

placed her where her back was against the wall, it gave her a view of the beach and allowed her to watch who came and went.

She was only half-way through her first donut when Amber and Josh arrived. Murdoch heard Amber introduce Josh. Moments later Amber came to the table, while Josh ordered and flirted with Harriet.

When Amber sat down, she asked, "Is it just me or is Harriet a bit, I don't know, distant, cold, stand-offish?"

Murdoch glanced back at the counter. "Yeah, I'm not sure what the word is either, but I do know something's off. Though she seems to like Josh." She shrugged and brought her attention back to Amber, who said, "There were two bodies in the warehouse."

Murdoch took a deep breath. "Not surprising. Sailor and Curly?"

"Probably. We won't know until after the autopsy. That's assuming the Medical Examiner can verify their identities. The bodies were pretty badly burned."

"Well, Smith did say he thought he knew who the two were and he only wanted Terri to verify his suspicions." Murdoch looked around to make sure there wasn't anyone close enough to overhear them. "He probably had them tied up somewhere in the back; it was a big warehouse. Once he got her confirmation, she was part of the same loose end, as they were."

Josh arrived at the table, smiling. He sat down next to Amber. After distributing the food and beverages he looked at Amber and asked, "Is Harriet single?"

Amber's eyebrows went up as she looked from him to Murdoch and back. "You sure work fast. Yes, she's single."

He turned and looked at Harriet. Amber touched his arm to get his attention. Then she said, "She's also my friend. Hurt her and I'll hurt you."

"Message received."

Murdoch asked, "Now that the Dating Game is over, can we get back to business? What's the plan for catching Mr. Smith in the act?"

"According to Terri, the girls are brought to Buckles Park, just above the beach where Edith Bates killed that girl. They move them down to the beach and onto Zodiacs, which then transport them out to a ship that's waiting beyond the twelve-mile mark." She took a swallow of coffee. "It's a good plan. Keeps them from having to bring the ship into a port where someone might want to inspect it and as long as they don't enter U. S. waters the Coast Guard can't board them." She paused and looked around. "Damn, I'm going to miss this place."

Josh quietly consumed his order of Madeleines and tea, while listening to Amber and Murdoch.

Murdoch chuckled. "Yeah sure, with all the restaurants and such in DC, you're going to miss My Place?"

Amber smiled. "I'm a simple girl. All those ethnic restaurants and fancy nightclubs, not really my style."

"When is this transfer supposed to take place?"

"Tomorrow night. The ship was delayed by bad weather, or the girls would already be gone."

CHAPTER 20

LC listened to the phone on the other end ringing. Just as she was about to disconnect Sara picked up.

"Hello."

"Hi Sara. How're you doing?"

"I'm doing okay. What's up?"

"I was wondering if you might like a day at the beach."

LC could hear the smile in her voice. "Of course, I'd love a day at the beach. I'm working today but I'm off tomorrow."

"What time do you get off today?"

"Five."

"Why don't you go home after work, grab a few things, and come over? By the time you hit the road rush hour should be over."

There was a brief pause. "Sounds like a plan to me."

"I'll text you the address."

LC rubbed Tuts ears. "Company coming tonight, little man."

Around nine that night when Sara pulled into the driveway tripping the security lights, LC was in her favorite spot watching the ocean and listening to her new police scanner. It was a quiet night, not much going on in the small town of Coventry Beach.

LC watched the older model Camaro on her monitor, wondering when Sara was going to emerge.

Sara sat in the car wondering if she was underdressed. She hadn't been expecting quite such a beach *house*. Cargo shorts, a t-shirt from the most recent Melissa Etheridge concert, and sandals completed her outfit.

I expected an apartment, or a timeshare, but not a house. Wonder if she owns it or if it's just a vacation lease.

She opened the car door, dropped her sandals to the ground, and slipped them on as she stood up. and reached behind the driver's seat for her overnight bag.

As soon as Sara shut the car door, LC closed her laptop and moved to the front door. With a smile on her face and Tut draped around her neck she greeted Sara, "Welcome. Come on in." She stood aside allowing Sara in.

The warm smile on LC's face dispelled any concerns she had about her attire.

"That's an interesting fashion accessory."

"I've found that he's less likely to try and run out the door if I have him up here." She rubbed the top of the cat's head. "Can I get you something to drink? Soda? Beer? Wine? Coffee? Tea? Water? I also have a variety of hard liquor."

"A beer, please." She checked out the house as she followed LC to the kitchen. "Is this your place?"

LC knew that it would be easy enough to catch her in the lie, but she told it anyway. "A friend of mine is letting me stay here, while I think through some things."

Sara accepted the beer and stepped out onto the screened in lanai.

"Thanks. That's some friend."

The ocean was calm as a lake and the full moon spread a path of silver from where it was coming over the horizon to the shore. LC came out behind her and closed the slider most of the way, leaving just enough room for Tut to come and go.

LC moved past Sara to her preferred chair. "Please, have a seat. Just know that Tut may decide to join you in whichever chair you choose."

Sara sat down and nodding toward the scanner asked, "Why the scanner? I wouldn't expect a lot of crime in this area."

LC reached over and turned the scanner off. Shrugging she said, "No, not much crime. I just like to know what's going on."

The two women sat in silence for a few minutes.

"Sorry I wasn't able to meet you and Elizabeth for dinner the other night."

"No problem but you know we really didn't expect you to pick up the tab."

LC shrugged. "No worries. I felt guilty after saying I'd be there and then not showing." She took a long swig from her beer, stood up, and said, "How about a walk on the beach?"

"Sure." Sara started to take off her sandals.

"You might want to leave those on until we get to the beach. The path can be unfriendly to bare feet." LC looked around and saw Tut giving himself a bath, sitting on one of the bar stools. "Are you coming with us?"

He looked up at her and then returned to his grooming.

"I guess not."

They left their shoes at the end of the path and walked through the soft sand to the hardpack. LC led them out to where the waves would wash over their feet.

Walking where the waves lapped against their ankles the two women enjoyed the soft sounds of the gentle surf in silence.

After a while Sara quietly asked, "What was her name?"

The question took LC by surprise. "I'm not sure what you mean."

"Really?"

LC sighed and as they walked the words came out of her, like water through a broken dam. "Her name was Rachel. We had seven glorious years together." She stopped and turned to face Sara. "And then she died."

Sara reached out and touched LC's arm. "I'm so sorry. That must have been devastating."

Prompted by questions from Sara, LC talked about her life with Rachel.

Back at the house, as they stepped into the lanai, LC said, "You do know I didn't invite you over here to get you into bed."

"Seriously? I was under the impression that this was a, what do they call it these days, I know it used to be called a bootie call."

The look on LC's face was too much and Sara laughed. "Even if that had been your intention, it wasn't mine."

CHAPTER 21

LC woke just before sunrise and headed downstairs. The smell of fresh brewed coffee greeted her as she descended the stairs.

Sara must be an early riser too.

Coffee in hand, she stepped onto the lanai. "Good morning. Thanks for making the coffee."

Sara took in a deep breath of the damp, salty air. "Good morning. You're welcome. Thank you for making it possible for me to sit here and enjoy this" she indicated the beach with the sun just beginning to peak over the horizon.

The two women sat in companionable silence and watched the sun lay a ribbon of gold across the calm water. The few clouds present turned from pastel pinks and lavenders to scarlet and purple, eventually becoming puffs of white cotton.

LC turned on the white noise app. Sara looked at her in surprise. "The sound of the real ocean isn't enough for you?"

"What can I say, I like white noise." For several more minutes they watched the waves, the sea gulls, and the pelicans.

"You're a very lucky woman, Larissa Carpenter."

LC gave a small laugh. "How long have you known?"

"Last night, after I went to my room. I searched the property appraiser's site." She smiled. "I wanted to know who this *friend* of yours was."

Tut wandered out and jumped onto LC's lap. She petted the cat saying, "Yes, your majesty. I'll get up and get your breakfast." She looked at Sara. "And then we're going out for breakfast."

CHAPTER 22

LC held the door to My Place open for Sara. Seeing Harriet behind the counter, she called out, "Good morning, Harriet."

Smiling Harriet's eyes moved from LC to Sara and back. "Good morning, chère."

"Harriet, I'd like you to meet Sara. Sara, Harriet makes the best beignets this side of New Orleans and her chicory coffee is divine."

"Nice to meet you, Sara."

"Pleasure to meet you, Harriet."

LC asked, "Sara, will you let me order for you?"

With a smile Sara nodded her agreement.

LC turned to Harriet. "Two chicory coffees and two orders of beignets and can we get one of your omelets to share." Looking around LC could see her favorite table was open and she asked Sara, "Why don't you go grab that table by the window before somebody else does?"

As if she knew that LC would want to sit with her back to the wall Sara left that seat for her.

Having each consumed their share of a bacon, onion, red pepper omelet, they were finishing off the last of the beignets when the door chimes sounded.

Murdoch was only a few feet from the door when LC leaned across the table, brushed her fingers gently down Sara's cheek, and gave her a soft kiss. "Thank you for last night."

LC's actions were observed by Harriet and Murdoch. Harriet quickly turned her attention to Murdoch, interested to see her reaction.

Murdoch paused for just an instant before continuing to the counter.

Harriet noticed that Murdoch's jaw muscle was jumping, and it made her smile. *Seems like the detective has taken too long to make a move on LC.* "Good morning detective."

Murdoch just nodded, cleared her throat, and said, "Two large black coffees. One dozen cake donuts, half with dark chocolate frosting, and half-a-dozen beignets. To go."

As Harriet moved around filling Murdoch's order she said, "Haven't seen Special Agent Hoffner or her partner in here since the other day. Is everything all right? She hasn't gone and got herself shot again, has she?"

"No, she and her partner are both doing fine. Busy with the case is all."

Harriet placed the coffee cups in a carrier next to the bag of goodies. "Well, I'm glad to hear that. You tell them I was asking about them."

Murdoch handed Harriet some money and picked up her purchases. "Will do. Keep the change."

LC's eyes followed every move Murdoch made. Her attention to the detective didn't escape Sara's notice.

"So, I take it she's the reason for the police scanner?"

Realizing how obvious she had been, LC blushed. "Yeah, I suppose she is."

"Want to talk about it?"

"Not really."

CHAPTER 23

Murdoch was driving on autopilot as her mind kept replaying the scene at My Place.

Over and over, she saw LC's fingers brush down the woman's cheek as she leaned across the table and gently kissed her before thanking her for the previous night.

Stop it! There could be any number of reasons to thank someone for… Who the hell am I kidding? That thank you was for one thing and one thing only. Damn it!

Murdoch had just passed the first entrance to the semi-circular driveway when she spotted the Happy Birthday balloons tied to the mailbox. She checked her rearview mirror and since no one was coming up behind her, she pulled past the second entrance a bit and backed into the driveway. Amber's government issued SUV was nowhere to be seen.

Probably put it in the garage.

Murdoch left the engine running while she put the windshield sunshade in place. Remembering the forecast was zero percent chance of rain for the day, she lowered each window about a half inch. Since her car would be visible from the house she felt the risk of leaving the windows cracked was acceptable, especially considering the heat.

She killed the engine on the car and opened the door. The wave of hot moist air slammed into her and took her breath away.

One of these days I'm going to get used to this place.

She grabbed the drink holder with the two coffees and placed it on the roof of the car before closing the driver's side door and opening the back door. She hung the plastic bag with the paper plates, napkins, and disposable utensils on her left arm, and grabbed the bag with the boxes of goodies from My Place. She used her foot to close the door, grabbed the coffees from the roof, and headed for the house.

At the front door she rang the bell and waited, as she felt the tickle of sweat rolling down her chest.

Patience was not one of Murdoch's virtues and already being agitated by LC, then missing the driveway, and now this sauna like heat, her fuse was reaching its end.

Amber started for the door as soon as the doorbell rang; however, when she opened the door to Murdoch, she realized she hadn't been fast enough. Murdoch's arm was raised, her hand fisted, and in position to pound on the door.

Amber smiled. "Can you say impatient?"

Murdoch dropped her arm back to her side, pushed past Amber, and headed to the kitchen.

The cool air inside the house helped ease Murdoch's heat induced agitation; however, it didn't do anything at all for the LC induced agitation.

A few feet down the open passage that led to the kitchen, Murdoch stopped. She tilted her head back to savor the cool air blowing from the vent above her.

Amber waited behind her. Though they hadn't known each other long, she knew there was something besides the summer heat that had riled up Murdoch.

She watched Murdoch drop her head forward allowing the cold air to hit the back of her neck. Five seconds later she was on the move again, headed to the kitchen.

"I take it I'm the first to arrive."

"Yes. Josh is on his way. He's stopping at South Cove Beach Police Department to pick up Carlton and two others."

"Carlton. Does he give you the same…? The same what?" Murdoch sighed. "I don't even know how to describe it. I just know the man has it in for me." She shrugged. "And I can't think of what I've done to him."

"I know what you mean about how he acts toward you. I mean, he's not all buddy-buddy with me, but at the same time I don't get that he – dislikes me the way he does you."

Murdoch set out the paper plates, napkins, and utensils before opening the boxes of goodies from My Place.

She started to reach for a beignet but decided she didn't want to have to deal with confectioners' sugar on her clothes and opted for two cake donuts instead. One with chocolate frosting and one without.

The smell of fresh brewed coffee drew her to the other end of the counter where Amber had made a pot.

Instead, of pouring a cup, Murdoch grabbed one of the cups she'd brought from My Place. She removed the top, opened the refrigerator freezer, and set the cup on the shelf below the bag of ice Amber had placed there earlier.

"Too bad it's such a small freezer. I could be tempted to get in if it were a little bigger."

Laughing Amber said, "I'm afraid it would need to be quite a bit bigger for either of us to get in."

Murdoch pointed to the boxes from My Place. "You better get what you want now. Cause once the boys arrive that stuff will disappear."

"Too true." Amber grabbed a plate and a cake donut with dark chocolate frosting. Like Murdoch she wanted a beignet but didn't want to deal with the confectioners' sugar.

While she nibbled on her donut Murdoch looked over the house. Her eyes moved from the oak cabinets to granite counter tops to the island in the middle of the spacious kitchen. The family room with the fireplace had the curtains drawn against anyone who happened to wander onto the property. Yet the room was well-lit. Murdoch's eyes moved up and noticed two sun tunnels in the room. The open floor plan, light colored wood flooring made the place feel larger than it was.

Amber had already set up the folding chairs, the table, and the screen for the projector. On the table, the projector was attached to a laptop. Ready to go.

It crossed Murdoch's mind that this was a place LC would like.

"Damn it!" She yanked open the freezer door, grabbed her coffee cup, to which she added a handful of ice cubes. Then she slammed the door.

"Wow! What has you so pissed off?"

Murdoch took a deep, calming breath, at least it was supposed to help calm her. It didn't really work.

"What are you talking about?

'You swear as if someone just slapped you and then take it out on the freezer. What's going on?"

"I don't want..." Murdoch sighed. "How well did you know LC in high school?"

"She and I were lab partners in science class. We didn't socialize outside of school or in school for that matter." Amber gripped the counter edge behind her with both hands. "What's she done that has you so twisted?"

"Twisted. Yeah, that's a good word for it." She sighed and looked directly at Amber. "And the truth is, I don't know why. I have zero right to be jealous."

Murdoch outlined the scene at My Place between LC and the unknown woman.

Smiling, Amber shook her head. "Man, you've got it bad. I don't know what to tell you other than to talk to her." Murdoch started to interrupt. "And I don't mean about any of the cases. I mean talk to her about the two of you."

"There is no 'two of us'."

The doorbell rang. Amber started toward the front door, turned, and said, "Then you better get over being jealous."

CHAPTER 24

The doorbell was Josh and the two detectives from South Cove Beach Police Department.

"Welcome gentlemen and lady."

"Special Agent Hoffner meet Detectives Gooden and Wilder." Josh's eyes moved from Wilder to Gooden as he continued, "Special Agent Hoffner is in charge of this operation."

Amber shook Det. Gooden's hand and then directed him to the kitchen, where there were snacks and coffee available. Gooden smiled and headed for the kitchen.

Even though they hadn't been working together long, Josh had already learned to read some of Amber's silent signals. He had a feeling she wanted a chance to talk to Wilder, alone.

He looked at Amber and asked, "Are any of those snacks from My Place?"

Amber smiled. "Yes."

"Excuse me ladies. I hear a Beignet calling my name."

"Det. Wilder, it's nice to meet you." She looked around the room. Once she was certain that no one was close enough to overhear their conversation she continued, "How does Det. Carlton treat you?"

Wilder smiled. "You cut right to the chase, don't you?"

87

"When necessary, yes."

"About what you'd expect from a Neanderthal." She shrugged. "But he doesn't get in my way. He doesn't consider me worth the bother."

A slow smile turned up the corners of Amber's mouth. "Thank you." She paused. "Better get some coffee while there's still some to be had."

That's why he doesn't like Murdoch. She's experienced. She's solved complex cases without the help of a man. I've seen Wilder's record. She's a newly minted detective. He doesn't consider her a threat. At least not yet.

The next arrival was Chief Warrant Officer Phillips of the U. S. Coast Guard.

Shortly after Phillips, Carlton arrived, and Amber decided it was time to get down to business.

"Welcome to Operation Surfs Up." Amber started the PowerPoint, which displayed a diagram of Buckles' Park parking lot. In the center of the lot was a concrete block building that held the restrooms. The Men's room was on the south side of the building and the Ladies was on the north side.

"Team Two will be Special Agent Robertson, Det. Gooden, and Det. Wilder. Special Agent Robertson will be lead on Team Two." She paused. "Team One, will be myself, Det. Murdoch, and Det. Carlton."

Det. Carlton interrupted. "I have a question. Murdoch's not FBI and this operation isn't in her jurisdiction so, why is she involved?"

Amber looked around the room at the other male officers. Their faces were closed, leaving her no way to tell where they stood on the issue Carlton had raised. Locking eyes with Carlton, she said, "This is a multi-jurisdictional case. Some aspects of it have taken place in Coventry Beach, others in South Cove. Det. Murdoch is part of Operation Surfs Up because I'm the agent in charge and I say she's in." She looked around the room. "Anyone else have something to say."

Amber took a deep breath and returned to the briefing. "Since both Team One and Two will be blind to the parking lot activity, there will be a spotter in the north dunes. Once they see where the truck is parked, we'll know exactly which of the two plans to initiate."

Amber started to speak but Det. Carlton cut her off. "Who's the spotter? I like to know who I'm working with."

"Our spotter is an experienced FBI agent and that's all you need to know about them." She held Carlton's gaze for several seconds before she turned her attention to Chief Warrant Officer Phillips. "We don't know how many ZODIACs will be arriving to pick up this group because we don't know how many people we're talking about. I'd like for you to have half of your team in the dunes to the south and half in the dunes to the north." Amber paused. "I don't want those boats leaving with or without any of the victims. How you stop them is entirely up to your team." She smiled. "However, I would like to have someone to interrogate when this is over."

Phillips nodded and smiled. He hadn't been particularly in favor of having his men involved in this operation when it was presented to him. In previous joint operations there was always too much politics involved. They wanted to put restrictions on his team. But he was warming to this operation.

Stopping assholes without having our hands tied. Works for me.

"Team Two, will be in the Men's room. If the truck parks on the north end of the parking lot, two of you will go to the right and come around the building to the truck. I want one of each side of the truck's cab and the third will exit to the left and head toward the ramp. Robertson, since you're in charge of Team Two. You decide who goes where."

"Got it."

"I'll be leading Team One." Amber turned her eyes to Det. Frank Carlton. "This is a multiple agency operation and the better we cooperate with each other the safer the operation will be for all concerned, including the captives."

She moved her gaze back to the image on the screen. "My team, will come out and start separating the victims from the men moving them."

Det. Frank Carlton asked, "Why do you keep calling them men? Isn't it possible that some of them will be women?"

Amber turned back toward the detective. "It is, possible, though statistics show that approximately 75% of human traffickers are men."

Refusing to get drawn into an argument with Carlton, she returned to the matter at hand. "No matter how much planning we do, an operation like this is unpredictable. There are too many moving variables, most of them human, to know exactly how things will go down."

Amber looked out over the group of all men, except for Murdoch and Detective Wilder, knowing that at least half of them were hoping this operation would fail, just so she would look bad. She didn't think they would do anything intentional, but they would be happy to see her fail. Especially, Det. Frank Carlton.

"If the truck parks to the south, the assignments are simply reversed for Teams One and Two." She paused. "Also, as soon as the shooting stops, assuming there is resistance, there will be an FBI film crew on hand to video the aftermath."

What she didn't tell anyone was that as soon as the truck was spotted two video drones would be launched to film everything. From the arrival of the truck or trucks, through as much of the operation as the drones had power for.

Chief Warrant Officer Phillips stood up. "That creates a problem for my team. I can't have them filmed."

Amber smiled. "I had a feeling you might take issue with the filming. Have your men wear masks." She handed him a small box. "Inside, are red number pins. Have each man attach one to his uniform, where it can easily be seen. Once you've assigned the pins, give me a list with the correct number next to each man's name."

Phillips looked confused.

Amber continued, "With an operation this size, I have to be able to account for the actions of each person involved. If I can't see their faces, I have to have a way to ID who did what."

Phillips nodded his head, gave Amber a mock salute, and sat back down.

"Does anyone else have any questions?"

CHAPTER 25

Word came from the spotter that the truck was parked on the north side of the restrooms.

"Have they unloaded their cargo?" Amber asked.

"No. There are three of them and they're standing by the back of the truck looking out to sea."

Amber hated the waiting. The anticipation of danger bothered her far more than the danger itself. Once things were happening, she knew what to do. Waiting was painful.

Then she heard in her earpiece. "One of them has moved off from the truck. He's near the railing at the north end." There was silence for a moment. "Looks like he's just lighting up. Wait. The other two are… Yes, they're unlocking the back of the truck."

The wait was over. "All units go."

Team Two raced out of the men's room. FBI Special Agent Josh Robertson and South Cove Beach Police Department Detective Gooden turned to the right and went around the west side of the building. Josh went around the front end of the truck to the passenger side. Then Det. Gooden ran to the driver's side.

Detective Wilder turned left and went around the east side of the building and stationed herself at the top of the ramp that led to the beach.

When Team One came out of the Women's Room, Detective Frank Carlton took up a position near Det. Wilder at the top of the ramp. Amber and Murdoch ran for the men at the back of the truck. The two men near the truck surrendered quickly.

Out of the corner of her eye Murdoch saw the third man jump the railing into the dunes.

"Hoffner, you got these two?" Murdoch was already headed for the railing as Amber confirmed she had the two suspects.

At the railing Murdoch paused, looking for the man who had jumped. The muzzle flash from his gun told her exactly where he was.

Having landed in the soft sand of the dunes Lawrence Philpot had trouble getting his footing. He rolled over on his back and when he saw Murdoch at the railing he fired. Murdoch returned fire, rapidly getting off two rounds. Her assailant fired a second round, but it went wide and hit her left arm.

Three ZODIACs beached, two men in each one. They came ashore with their automatic weapons slung over their shoulders.

The sound of gunfire from the park had them each reaching for their weapons, but it was too late.

"Hands up and face down in the sand, now!" The authoritative voice came from the dunes.

Each of the men noticed the red dots on their chests and began to surrender. Except for one man, who threw himself to the sand, rolled away from the others, propped himself up on his elbows, and pulled his AK-47 around from his back. A single shot rang out and his head dropped onto his rifle in the sand.

The six U. S. Coast Guard Maritime Security Response Team members emerged from the dunes, dressed in desert camouflage. In the dim light the sand falling from them gave them an eerie, ghost-like appearance.

Chief Warrant Officer Phillips removed the weapons from each of their captives and zip tied their hands behind their backs, while his men continued to keep a weapon locked on each one.

Phillips quickly determined the leader of the group and took him aside. "We don't have a lot of time here. What I want to know is this, would you prefer to do time in a Federal prison here in the states or somewhere less pleasant?"

The man stared at him for several seconds, saying nothing. "Like I said, I don't have a lot of time, so you either decide to help me or I'll get one of your friends over there to help me. Your choice."

The man remained stone faced and silent. Phillips looked over the group of men sitting in the sand. He had a real knack for sizing a man up at a glance. "That's fine sucker, I'll take the skinny little guy on the end over there. He'll tell me what I want to know and the rest of you can deal with the FBI and Homeland." Phillips started to walk away.

"Wait!" He licked his lips. "What do you want to know?"

"I want the name of and the coordinates of the ship where you were going to deliver your human cargo."

The man licked his lips again and stepped closer to Phillips. His voice was almost a whisper. "If I cooperate you have to give me protection. You don't know these people. I'll never be safe in any prison."

Phillips maintained his poker face. "I'll put in a good word and if you're information is valid and shows results, I'm sure we can work something out."

Once Phillips had the information, he returned his informant to the group of prisoners sitting on the beach.

Phillips and all but one of his men, who was left to guard the prisoners, huddled together.

By the time Amber came down to the beach to see the handiwork of the Coast Guard team, Phillips had a plan in place.

Looking around at the scene she quickly assessed the situation, three ZODIACs, five prisoners and one fatality. "Chief Phillips, looks like you and your men did a good job here."

Phillips wasn't one to give away anything with a facial expression, now was no exception. "Yes ma'am. We also have the name and coordinates of the ship they were supposed to transport the cargo to."

Smiling Amber said, "Please, tell me it's inside U.S. waters."

"I wish."

Amber's smile disappeared but as she studied Phillips' face, it began to return. "You have a plan. Talk to me."

CHAPTER 26

Sitting in the back of the open ambulance Murdoch watched the organized chaos in front of her.

She paid particular attention to the film crew Amber had requisitioned. There were three guys with high-end video cameras filming all the activity in the park. From the EMT that was wrapping her arm to the captives being carefully placed in patrol cars to be driven to the hospital for evaluation, they were catching it all on video. The video was not only being saved to the memory of each camera, but it was also being simultaneously uploaded to a secure cloud account. There were two more cameramen down on the beach filming.

Amber came up the ramp from the beach and stepped up next to Murdoch. Looking at the bullet lodged in Murdoch's vest she said, "You're going to need a new vest."

"Yeah, I guess so." Murdoch stared at the bullet embedded in her vest, thinking how without the vest this could have had a different ending. "How did things go on the beach?"

"Chief Warrant Officer Phillips and his men did a great job, and they have a plan to bring the mother ship into U.S. waters."

The media vans were clogging the street outside the park and anyone living in the nearby houses was no doubt fuming

96

about the law enforcement and media circus happening in the park.

Those people aren't getting any sleep tonight. It'll be daybreak before all this is cleared out of here.

The EMT working on her arm said, "You should really go to the hospital and have that looked at."

Murdoch stood up and rolled her shoulders back. The action caused pain in her left arm where the bullet had gone through, and she winced. "Yeah, I probably should but…"

"…but nothing. You're going to the hospital and getting checked out. There's nothing more for you to do here anyway." Amber directed her words to the EMT. "As soon as your partner gets that stretcher with Captive Number 5 loaded, Det. Murdoch will be riding to the hospital with you."

Murdoch started to speak but Amber cut her off. "I don't want to hear it. Bad enough you got injured on my watch. I'm not going to be responsible for complications because you wanted to hang around and be part of the action."

Amber started to walk away, then with a smile she turned, and said, "Thanks for all your help, Murdoch."

CHAPTER 27

Darkness was just beginning to fall as Sara and LC enjoyed an after-dinner tea on the lanai. Tut was on Sara's lap, which amused LC. It was nice that Tut approved of Sara. In LC's mind animals were incredibly good judges of people.

Though she dreaded the answer, LC asked, "Do you have work tomorrow?"

Sara sighed. "Sadly, yes." Absentmindedly rubbing Tut's head and staring out to sea, she continued, "Actually, I should probably head home tonight." Her words said she needed to leave but her voice said she wanted to stay.

LC felt deflated. She took a deep breath. "I'd really like for you to stay the night again." Her words came out quickly. "It's just nice to have someone around besides" she pointed at Tut "him."

"Sure. As long as you make sure I'm up and out of here by six."

"No problem. Walk on the beach?"

"Yes." Looking at Tut, Sara said, "I'm afraid you're going to have to let me up, you little beast."

Tut looked up at her and blinked.

LC picked up the cat's harness. "You want to go with us this time?"

The cat stretched and with the grace only a cat has, moved off Sara's lap to sit in front of LC. She slipped the harness on the feline, attached the retractable leash, and stood up.

Sara shook her head.

"What?"

With laughter in her voice Sara said, "I've just never seen a cat walked on a leash."

"If you think that's something, wait until we get down to the beach."

* * *

Rita listened to the exchange between the two women with keen interest. She was delighted that, for a change, the sound was coming through clearly. She had already chastised Michael regarding the sporadic reception, certain that he hadn't properly installed the bug.

Checking her watch, she decided that she could fix herself a quick snack while she waited for Sara and LC to return from their walk.

CHAPTER 28

Apart from their laughter at Tut's antics, the two women walked along in silence for several minutes.

Sara broke the silence. "What's the deal between you and the detective?" LC gave her a look, that said she didn't want to talk about it.

"Look you said you wanted someone to talk to besides the cat. So, talk."

Looking out to sea LC started. "I'm sure that even over in Central City you heard about the woman found on the shore here and then a short time later another woman was found dead down in South Cove Beach."

"Yeah. I remember hearing about all of that."

LC stopped and turned to face Sara. "I found the first body and they've never found the killer."

Sara looked into LC's eyes as she processed this information. "Okay, so you found the body."

LC laughed and started walking again. "Don't you know that the first people on every cop's suspect list are the person who finds the body and the spouse?"

Sara reached out and touched LC's arm. LC stopped again and faced her. "Seriously, the cops think you killed this woman. Did you know her? What do they think is your motive?"

"No, I didn't know her. I met her that morning when she was sneaking around on the path between the front of the house and the path to the beach."

As they walked along the shore Sara asked questions and LC answered them.

Tut wore himself out chasing after sand crabs and LC draped him around her neck for the last leg of the walk back to the house.

"Okay, let me see if I understand this – mess." Sara took a deep breath. "You spend some time talking to a woman claiming to be the niece of the former homeowner. She leaves you and heads down to the beach. That evening you find her body on the beach. The cops question you and you tell them what little you know."

"Very succinct summary."

"Then while sitting on your balcony you see a woman stab a man, while another woman watches. The two women leave him there. You call Det. Murdoch. The police come out and find the dead man. Again, you give them a statement and this time you provide sketches of the two women." Sara shakes her head in disbelief.

"Then while you and a former classmate along with her supposed fiancé are having dinner at your house with Det. Murdoch and Harriet from My Place, Murdoch gets notified of another dead woman on the beach. This time it's in South Cove Beach, just a few miles south of here." Sara paused to catch her breath.

"You're doing good. Keep going. I'm hoping that you'll find some nugget in all this that I've missed. Something that will help me figure out what's going on."

"Sure. So, Edith Bates, the woman who stabbed the man comes after you for telling the cops what you saw, and it turns out she's also the one who killed the woman down in South Cove. Murdoch ends up killing Bates in your kitchen. Your former classmate gets shot by a man working with Bates, and she in turn shoots and kills him. It turns out the classmate and her fiancé are both FBI agents. Did I miss anything?"

"Just that the man who was helping Edith Bates was Alan Henry, the man who had kidnapped Harriet."

"Oh yeah, right."

LC sighed. "That's basically my life since I moved here."

Sara laughed. "Girl, sell this place and get the hell out of Dodge."

"Don't think I haven't thought about it." She paused. "However, I doubt the police would be happy about me leaving the area."

"Why?" Then it hit Sara, she stopped LC at the bottom of the path back to the house. "You're kidding? They think that you're involved in the first killing. The one they haven't solved yet?"

LC gave a laugh and a sad smile. "Murdoch claims that she and FBI Special Agent Hoffner don't think I am, but that since the FBI hasn't cleared me, I'm still a person of interest."

The two women walked up the sandy path toward the house and Sara pondered LC's last statement.

As they entered the lanai Sara said, "You're not staying because you're a suspect. You're staying because you have a thing for Murdoch."

LC spun around to face her. "Why would you think that?"

Laughing Sara replied, "She's hot and now I understand what the 'thank you for last night' and the kiss were all about. You wanted her to see that. You wanted to make her jealous."

"You're crazy." LC refused to meet Sara's inquisitive gaze.

The police scanner erupted with an adrenaline-charged voice.

LC recognized the voice, FBI Special Agent Amber Hoffner was requesting multiple ambulances. "We have an officer injured, multiple suspects, and one fatality."

"No!" LC screamed as she staggered to her chair.

Tut climbed down from her neck and onto her lap. He pushed on her hand with his head, and she began to pet him.

Sara knelt next to LC's chair. "Are you alright?" She paused and waited for a response. "LC. Larissa."

"What? I...I'm sorry. It's just that – the voice on the scanner..." She paused, shook her head, and audibly swallowed. "It...it was Amber. The FBI agent I was telling you about. They're working a case together."

"They? Oh yeah, Murdoch."

LC nodded.

Sara pulled a chair over and sat down facing LC. "First, she said the officer involved was wounded, not dead. Plus, if it's a big case and it probably is, since the FBI is involved, I'm sure there are other cops there. It could have been anyone. It might not have even been a local officer. It could have been an FBI agent."

LC considered this hypothesis for a moment. "She said 'officer' not agent. Still, you're right that there are probably other officers involved." LC grabbed her cell phone. "And I know just the person to tell me who and how badly."

Susie Conklin's cell phone buzzed in her pocket. She looked at the screen and then accepted the call. "You do know I'm right in the middle of the biggest story this one-horse town has ever seen, right?"

"What I know Ms. Conklin, is that you want me to keep providing you with exclusives, right? Like an interview with the FBI agent in charge of the operation."

Susie wasted no time in asking, "What can I do for you Ms. Carpenter?"

"For starters you can tell me which officer was injured and how badly."

"We're still being kept out of the park. I know there was a call about an officer being injured but I...Wait a minute." She turned to her cameraman. "Zoom in on the back of that ambulance. Yeah, that one, where they're loading the stretcher."

LC's breath caught. *A stretcher.* She could still hear Susie talking to her cameraman.

"Thanks, Will. That's great footage."

Just as LC was about to lose her patience, Susie returned to their conversation. "Murdoch was helping load a stretcher into an ambulance and she has a bandage around her left arm. I think she got into the ambulance that's headed to the hospital. I've gotta go." The call ended.

If she was helping load a stretcher her injury can't be too bad.

104

Breathing a sigh of relief, LC caught the tail end of a phone conversation Sara was having.

"Yeah, I came over to the beach to visit a friend and now my car won't start. I'll get it looked at in the morning. If I can make it before the end of the day I will. It depends on what's wrong with it."

* * * *

An unpleasant smile spread across Rita Simmons face. She took a sip of her Chardonnay, dabbed her mouth with the linen napkin, and texted FBI Supervising Agent Michael Goldman.

"Need all details of tonight's operation in Buckle's Park and everything you can get on Det. Angela Murdoch. Immediately!!"

CHAPTER 29

Chief Warrant Officer Phillips' plan was simple. He and his men were going to use one of the ZODIACs and head out to the Mary Louise, lure the ship into U.S. waters, and board her.

They were two miles from the coordinates of the Mary Louise, when Phillips cut the motor on the ZODIAC.

"All right, Mr. Green. It's time for your performance."

Green took a deep breath, once again deciding whether to play ball with the Feds and face the consequences of Mr. Smith finding out or tell the Mary Louise to run for it the Coast Guard was waiting to board them.

"Mary Louise, this is Green. We ran into some trouble on shore. We were ambushed. I got away and I have some of the cargo, but my engine just died and I'm drifting back to shore."

For several seconds, there was no response. "Captain Wainwright?"

"You know I'm not supposed to enter U.S. waters."

"Fine. What do you want me to do with the cargo? Throw it overboard? Cause I'm sure as hell not getting caught with it when I drift back to the beach. And you can explain to Mr. Smith what happened."

There was silence for a moment and then a new voice came over the phone. "Mr. Green, we're on our way. Do not, I repeat, do not dispose of my cargo."

"Yes, sir, Mr. Smith."

Phillips took the satellite phone from Mr. Green. "Now we wait."

Average speed of a cargo ship, approximate distance, they should be here in about ten minutes, maybe sooner. Phillips stared in the direction he expected the Mary Louise to come from.

He silently signaled his radioman to notify the Coast Guard Cutter that was waiting for their signal. The coded message went out and the wait continued.

With the tide pushing the ZODIAC closer to the shore, Phillips knew that when the Mary Louise arrived, she would be well inside U.S. waters.

CHAPTER 30

Heading for the beacon on the ZODIAC, the 140-foot trimaran, Mary Louise, crossed into U.S. waters.

The U.S. Coast Guard Cutter Freedom was running dark. With spotters using night vision binoculars fore, aft, and on both sides of the ship, Captain Buckner was still uneasy about maintaining a lights-off status.

Maintaining a half-mile distance between his ship and the Mary Louise, the Freedom followed in her wake. As soon as his radar operator announced that the Mary Louise was in U. S. waters, Buckner set a three-minute timer.

His timer went off. "All right, ladies and gentlemen, lights up and bring us within fifty yards of the target."

Coming up behind the Mary Louise, the dual spotlights of the Freedom shone on the ship. Buckner announced over the public address system, "This is the U.S. Coast Guard. Cut your engines and prepare to be boarded."

All eyes aboard the yacht turned to Mr. Smith, he sighed and nodded to the captain of his vessel. "Cut the engines and let them aboard." The muscles in his jaw were jumping. He drew in a deep breath, forced himself to relax, and said, "It would seem that Mr. Green has changed sides."

Every person within hearing knew those words were a death sentence for Eddie Green. Traitors were worth a quarter of a million dollars to the person who could provide proof of death to Mr. Smith.

Captain Buckner moved his ship into position and the Mary Louise was boarded without incident.

CHAPTER 31

Murdoch was in one of four curtained rooms in the ER. Deputy Miller was her assigned Gatekeeper. He was at his post outside her room.

As Gatekeeper, Miller's job was to restrict access to Murdoch. The forensics team, the Critical Incident Team, and medical personnel were the only people allowed access.

Waiting was never one of Murdoch's strong suits. Sitting on the exam table, she closed her eyes, took long steady breaths, and imagined herself walking on the beach.

She opened her eyes when she heard someone enter her space. She recognized the man. "CSI Walton."

"Detective Murdoch." He paused. "You know the drill." He handed her a brown paper bag. "Clothes in here." Then he gave her a box. "Gun in here. Let me know when I can come back in."

She unbuckled her belt and removed the holster holding her duty gun. It occurred to her that the most efficient thing would be to deal with boxing the gun now. Instead, she laid it on the exam table, where it was still accessible.

Then she removed the grey sweats from the bag, stripped, put the baggy, comfortable sweatpants on, stuffed her clothes into the paper bag, and placed the bag on top of her Kevlar vest. She studied the long sleeve, pull over sweatshirt. Before putting it on she located a pair of scissors and cut the left sleeve off, before putting the shirt on.

Finally, she opened the box and saw that there was a place in the form fitting foam inside for the 9mm and another spot for the clip. She put each item in its assigned location, closed the lid, and added her holster to the bag of clothes.

Murdoch took a deep breath and released it slowly. "Walton."

CSI Walton stepped back into the room. He moved the vest, the bag, and the gun box to a chair. Indicating the camera around his neck, "I need to get some shots of the wound. Any idea when the doctor's going to show up?"

A brusque young man pushed the curtain aside and entered. "Is now okay with you?"

Murdoch could tell Walton wasn't happy with the doctor's tone, but he maintained his professionalism. "I just need to photograph the detective's injuries."

Without a word the doctor unwrapped the bandage around Murdoch's upper left arm and stepped aside, allowing Walton to move in and take pictures of the gunshot wound.

While Walton was taking pictures, the doctor bagged the gauze bandage he'd removed from Murdoch's arm. When Walton stepped back from Murdoch the doctor handed him the bag containing the bandage.

Examining her wound the doctor said, "This is a clean, through and through, single gunshot wound. You were lucky. It didn't hit the bone. The EMT did a good job." He looked from the wound to Murdoch's face. "I understood you were shot twice. Was I misinformed?"

"No, you weren't." Murdoch reached up and rubbed the upper part of her sternum. "My vest took the brunt of that shot." Knowing the doctor would want to visually examine the area and Walton would need to photograph it, she pulled the sweatshirt off over her head.

Guess I'm not thinking too clearly, right now. I could have left that sleeve after all.

Considering his bedside manner, Murdoch was surprised at how gentle the doctor was when he touched the area of impact. "It doesn't appear that anything is broken but we'll do an x-ray to make certain." He indicated that Walton could take his photos.

When the CSI finished putting his camera away, he asked, "Anything I can get for you, Murdoch? Maybe someone you need to have called?"

Murdoch pulled the sweatshirt back on. "No. Thanks. I'm good."

"You take care. I'll be seeing you."

"Actually, there is something you could get for me. A note pad and a pen. I want to get some things written down, while they're still fresh."

He reopened his kit, pulled out the requested items. "I always have extras with me."

"Thanks."

Walton nodded and was gone.

When the doctor finished rebandaging her arm, he said, "Sit tight, detective. Someone will be around to take you for that x-ray."

Alone again, Murdoch began writing down everything she could remember about Operation Surfs Up, paying particular attention to the incident in the park. When she'd written everything she could think of, she returned to her meditation, which was quickly interrupted by a young woman pushing a wheelchair.

"I'm here to take you for your x-ray."

Murdoch wasn't happy about the wheelchair but knew that there was no use arguing about it. It was hospital policy, and the young woman had no authority to make an exception in her case.

Deputy Miller followed along behind the nurse, flirting the entire way.

The x-ray showed no fractures to the sternum.

Murdoch signed all the necessary forms to be released and the nurse at checkout handed her two prescriptions. "Doctor says you're to get these filled right away. He also says to keep taking the antibiotics until they're all gone." She paused and held Murdoch's gaze. "There's no telling where that bullet was before it went through your arm."

After getting the prescriptions filled Deputy Miller dropped Murdoch off at her place.

CHAPTER 32

LC tossed and turned most of the night and was up before sunrise. She made coffee and set out fruit. When Sara told her that she was going to stay another day, LC told her that it wasn't necessary. It had just been the initial shock. Sara informed her that she was going to stay anyway.

When Sara told her that she had called her employer and told him she wouldn't be in because of car trouble, LC tried not to let her disapproval show. Lying for any reason was a big no-no in LC's world.

Sara smiled. "Another day at the beach will do me good." She titled her head and looked at LC. "Besides, I think you need to have someone around" before LC could say anything, she added "and you didn't ask. I volunteered."

Tut jumped into LC's lap and settled down to grooming himself. LC removed her phone from its holster on her hip and opened an app before placing the phone on the small table between herself and the sliding glass doors.

Sara cocked her head, listening, and asked, "I'm going to ask you again, what's with the white noise?"

LC looked from the phone to Sara. "I use it to interfere with the listening device someone has planted here."

"What?!?

LC laughed. "Yes, well, evidently someone wants to know about what's going on here."

Sara frowned. "You didn't have that going last night when you heard about the incident with Murdoch."

"Yes, I know." LC sighed. "Not really happy about that but it's not like everyone who sees the two of us together hasn't figured out that I have feelings for the detective."

Sara stepped inside the house and moments later returned with a cup of coffee and a plate of fruit. "When did you find out about the bug? That is the proper term, isn't it?"

"Yes, it's the common word." She shrugged. "A couple of days ago. I swept the house and then sat down to think about how I would deal with it. I've no idea who planted it. The local cops? The FBI? Someone else? Other than last night, I've been selective about what I let them hear." She smiled. "They're probably going crazy trying to figure out why they can hear some conversations and not others."

The sun was just coming up over the horizon. A huge orange ball spreading a path of gold all the way to the sand. Not a cloud in the sky. At that moment, the sea breeze was quite refreshing, yet it was obvious that the day would quickly become hot and humid.

Sara took a sip of coffee. "You don't look like you slept at all."

"Gee thanks. You, on the other hand, look very well rested."

Sara took a deep breath of the salty air before responding. "I slept like the dead but I'm not in an emotional quandary."

LC sighed. "Such a fancy word."

Sara kept her eyes toward the ocean and smiled but made no response.

"It just dawned on me that we've spent quite a bit of time together and I know virtually nothing about you. Tell me about yourself."

"I don't like to talk about me."

LC straightened up in her chair. "You can either tell me about you or I can hire a private investigator" she shrugged "which I may do anyway."

Sara laughed. "That took long enough." She sipped her coffee and then brought her eyes to LC's. "I've spent two nights in your house. You've told me things that I'll bet a week's salary you haven't told anyone else, except maybe a therapist or Harriet. Now finally, you're getting around to wondering who I am."

"I'm usually a good judge of people and Tut likes you. But now it's time I knew more."

"Where should I begin?"

"The beginning is usually the best place; however, I don't think I'm interested in hearing about your life from birth. How about if I ask a few pertinent questions?"

Sara nodded her agreement.

"Have you ever been arrested?"

"No."

"Is that because you've never been caught or is it because you've never done anything to be arrested for?"

Sara laughed. "Prior to winning that jackpot, were you an attorney?"

"No and I'm the one asking questions. And you haven't answered my last one."

"Have I ever done anything I could have been arrested for? Hmmm...Probably but nothing too serious. A little pot smoking

116

in college. I may have even been stupid enough in my youth to drive after drinking a bit much. Fortunately, it never harmed anyone."

"How often do you lie to your boss?"

"What makes you think I lie to my boss?"

"So, you're telling me that if I try to start your car right now, it won't start."

Sara tossed LC the keys to her car. "Give it a shot."

"Fine. I will."

The two women walked around the house to the driveway. LC unlocked the Camaro and slid into the driver's seat. She put the key in the ignition. Before turning it, she looked up at Sara standing in the car's open doorway.

LC was torn between wanting to catch Sara in a lie and hoping that the woman was telling the truth. Holding Sara's gaze, LC turned the key. Nothing, but a faint clicking sound.

She removed the key, slid out of the car, and asked, "What did you do to the car?"

Sara smiled. "You're good. I disconnected the battery. I'm a lousy liar. So, when I told Mark my car wouldn't start, I had to be telling him the truth."

"What if he had asked what was wrong with the car?"

"I'd have said it was probably a problem with the battery."

"A problem you caused."

"Yeah" she shrugged "but he's not going to want the details. He just wants to know I'll be in tomorrow to meet with a new client."

"A new client? What kind of work do you do?"

"I'm a CFP, Certified Financial Planner."

LC looked from Sara to the car and back to Sara. "Are you good at your job?"

"Yes."

"Why aren't you driving a newer car? This thing has to be at least eight, maybe ten years old."

Sara took her car keys from LC. "Just because I have enough money to buy a new car doesn't mean I should." She looked lovingly at the black on black, rag top. "I like this car. It may not get the best gas mileage, but it's paid for and is quite reliable."

LC laughed and led the way back around the house.

CHAPTER 33

Being an early riser, Murdoch was up before the sun.
Normally her day started with a workout, which included a soft
sand run on the beach. Then a shower and head to the office.
However, the doctor made a point of telling her, no physical
exertion for at least a week.

Out loud to no one, "What the hell am I supposed to do?"

Murdoch sat alone in her rented house, wondering how long
it would take the FBI to complete the incident investigation.
Regardless of how long it took, she was happy the FBI was
conducting the investigation instead of South Cove Beach.
Even though Det. Frank Carlton wouldn't have been the one
running the investigation since he was part of Operation Surfs
Up. He still would have exerted pressure on the investigators.

Don't know why that man just doesn't like me.

She got up and started wandering through the house. In the
spare bedroom, she looked at the boxes she still hadn't
unpacked.

Yeah, I should deal with those. How long have I been here?

She did some quick calculations in her head. *A year? Is that
really possible? Damn.*

Instead, she wandered back to the front of the house and stood looking out the picture window in the living room. Usually, she was delighted that her yard maintenance was included in her rent, but not today.

If I had the equipment, I could be out there working in the yard. Except the doc said no physical exertion.

It was a nice neighborhood. Everyone maintained their yard and house. Nothing fancy. Just a nice quiet, family friendly street.

She sighed and out loud declared, "I can't just sit around here doing nothing. I've got to do something."

Murdoch grabbed her keys, got in her car, and headed to My Place.

When she arrived, Harriet had a line at the register and kept looking back to the kitchen with a worried expression.

Murdoch stepped behind the counter next to Harriet and watched her as she checked out two more customers. One paid with cash and the other with a credit card. Harriet watched Murdoch watching her but didn't say a thing. Finally, she asked, "Can I help you detective?"

Murdoch smiled. "No, but I can help you." She gently nudged Harriet, who moved aside allowing Murdoch access to the register.

Murdoch smiled at the customer and asked, "How was your meal today?"

"Delicious, as always."

Murdoch spoke to Harriet without turning to look at her. "Don't you have something in the kitchen you need to take care of?"

Harriet turned and without a word headed to the kitchen.

Murdoch bussed tables and ran the register through the morning rush. There were a few people left in the dining area, when Harriet emerged from the kitchen and found Murdoch sitting at her favorite table, drinking coffee.

Harriet sat down opposite her. "Thank you."

Murdoch smiled, sipped her coffee, and said, "You're welcome. Just know that I'm not going to be available much longer. As soon as the doctor releases me for duty, I'm gone."

Harriet sighed. "I really do need to hire someone."

"What's stopping you?"

"I've never hired anyone before." She leaned closer and quietly asked, "What if I hire the wrong person?" She leaned back in her chair. "I guess I didn't count on this place being so successful that I'd need to hire help."

Murdoch's gaze swept over the room, then she looked at Harriet. "Look at the people in the dining area and tell me if anyone of them would be a good hire for you."

Harriet turned her chair so that her back was to the window. After a quick look around the dining area, she looked at Murdoch and said, "No."

"Why not? What's wrong with either of the young people over there in the far corner?"

"They're tourists. I want someone who will be here for the long haul."

"Okay, so what's wrong with the fellow over there. The one in the purple shirt."

"He's a good customer but he's not a people person."

"How do you know that?"

"Like I said, he's a regular and even if he wasn't. Look at him, he's just closed off."

Murdoch gave a soft laugh. "You'll do fine hiring the right person. Just put a sign in the window or place an ad" she paused "or both."

Harriet sat back in her chair and studied Murdoch. "Where did you learn to work in a restaurant?"

Murdoch smiled. "I grew up doing this stuff. My parents had a small restaurant and we all worked there at one point or another."

"All?"

"Yes, my siblings and I bussed tables, seated customers, ran the register, and cooked as soon as we were old enough."

Smiling, Harriet asked, "With that family background, how did you end up a cop?"

Murdoch laughed. "I hated that restaurant." She sipped her coffee. "I didn't mind working in the restaurant. What I hated was the way it consumed every waking minute of my parent's lives. If they weren't at the place working, they were at home planning menus, or out shopping for the best deals on produce or whatever."

"Yes, having a restaurant, even a small café like this could cut into family time." She paused and looked out over the dining area again before turning back to Murdoch. "So, you traded one all-consuming career field for another one."

"Yeah, but I get to carry a gun." Murdoch smiled over her coffee cup.

CHAPTER 34

LC and Sara parked next to each other in My Place's parking lot. The Electric Storm Blue Prius V stood in stark contrast to the black-on-black muscle car with its top down.

They walked into the aroma filled café to find Murdoch at the register. LC paused for the briefest of moments before continuing through to her second favorite table. There was already a cup of coffee and a plate with two cake donuts sitting on her favorite table.

Sara suppressed a smile as she followed LC to the table. Once they were seated Sara leaned across the table and said, "You need to talk to her."

LC's answer was emphatic, "No!" She looked at Sara with pleading eyes. "You go order for us, please."

Before Sara could respond, Murdoch arrived with two black coffees. "Can I get either of you anything else?"

Sara looked past Murdoch at the menu board. "Yes, I'd like an order of beignets and an omelet with cheese, red peppers, and bacon."

Murdoch looked at LC. "And for you?"

LC smiled at Sara. "I'll help her with her order."

Murdoch did a smart about face and headed to the kitchen to give Harriet the order.

Harriet jumped at Murdoch's abrupt entrance. "Chère, you have to slow down before you give me heart failure."

"Need an order of beignets and a cheese, red pepper, and bacon omelet."

Harriet pursed her lips, and wiping her hands on her apron, she moved to the kitchen door, and looked out the window.

She turned and looked at Murdoch. "So that's the problem."

Murdoch looked down at her shoes and then brought her eyes to Harriet. "What is it about that woman that makes me so crazy? We've never so much as held hands but seeing her with…makes me…I don't know."

"Jealous?" Harriet moved to the stove to begin the omelet.

"No…maybe…I hate feeling like this."

Whisking eggs, she looked at Murdoch. "You two need a good talking to." She poured the eggs into the skillet. As she added the peppers and crumbled bacon, she continued, "Or even better you two need to talk to each other." Moments later she added the shredded Colby jack cheese and folded the eggs over.

Murdoch moved next to Harriet, snorted, and said, "Yeah, the last time I tried talking to her, I got told we needed to keep our relationship professional, cop and suspect."

Harriet placed fresh beignets on a plate and dusted them with confectioner's sugar. "Grab that raspberry sauce and put some in a small bowl."

Murdoch did as ordered and placed the bowl on the plate with the beignets.

"Maybe you should think about what you were saying to her when she shut you down. In the meantime, you can deliver this order."

The bell at the register rang. Murdoch smiled. "Saved by the bell. I'll take care of the register and you can deliver the order." With that Murdoch held open the door from the kitchen.

As she walked past Murdoch, "You can't hide forever."

As she set the plates on the table, Harriet said, "Morning, chère. Sara. What are you two ladies up to today?"

"Sara leaves for work in Central City after breakfast. I'll be heading back to the house." LC lowered her voice a bit. "Murdoch's working for you now?"

"She's on medical leave and sitting around the house with nothing to do was driving her crazy. Can I get you ladies anything else?"

"Some more coffee would be great."

"Coming right up." Harriet headed back to the kitchen. She paused by the register, indicated LC's table, and said, "They need more coffee" and then kept going into the kitchen.

Murdoch glared at Harriet's back.

Then she remembered seeing Harriet put a thermal carafe under the counter the other day. She found it, filled it with coffee from the pot that had just finished brewing, and sat it on the table between LC and Sara.

"Enjoy," she said as she spun around and headed back to the register to deal with a customer who had just entered to pick up a to go order.

LC looked at Sara who was watching Murdoch retreat.

"You feel sorry for her."

Sara turned back to LC. "I think she cares a great deal for you and you're using it against her." They consumed breakfast in silence.

Taking a sip of coffee, Sara glanced at the wall clock behind the cash register. "I should hit the road. Traffic will be a nightmare and Mark won't be happy with me if I'm late." She reached for her wallet.

"Don't bother. I'll take care of it." LC smiled. "I'm going to take her advice and enjoy the coffee."

LC stood up and gave Sara a less than platonic hug. "Text me when you're there, otherwise I'll worry."

Sara emitted a short laugh and said, "You really are evil."

CHAPTER 35

Sara texted that she had arrived at work safe and on time. LC appreciated the consideration. The drive between the coast and the middle of the state was a treacherous one. Between construction and crazy drivers there were fatalities, almost daily.

While Murdoch was busy with customers LC dropped thirty dollars on the table and slipped out the door.

At the house she sat on the lanai with Tut for a while and then a reminder popped up on her phone. Gun Range.

She had put it on the calendar to show up once a month. Like many skills, using a firearm safely and effectively, requires practice.

She locked the sliding glass door and put Tut in his favorite house chair. Then she unloaded the 9mm, left the action open, emptied both magazines, and packed everything into the tactical range bag.

Fifteen minutes later, LC entered the gun range and was delighted to find that she was the only one there.

She flashed her membership card to the Range Master and moved to her favorite lane. Placing the gun case on the bench she began unpacking.

Placing the sound deadening earmuffs around her neck, safety goggles on her face, LC then removed the 9mm from its padded pistol pocket and laid it on the bench next to the case. With practiced hands she used the speed loader to load both magazines.

She pressed the button to bring the target holder to her, placed her target, and sent it out thirty feet. With both hands around the butt of the pistol, her weapon safely pointed at the ceiling, LC looked around to make sure it was safe to fire.

She lowered her gun, finger outside the trigger guard, aimed at the target, and fired. Without changing targets, she emptied both magazines.

All sixteen rounds hit the Splatterburst Triple Silhouette target. Each bullet showed a bright neon yellow where it landed. Most of her shots were eights and nines, with a couple of tens that hit dead center.

LC had rented the lane for an hour; however, it only took her half that time to go through both magazines twice. Satisfied with her accuracy she packed up her gear, rolled up both targets she'd used, and headed home.

On the drive home, her mind wandered to thoughts of Murdoch. *Think I'll show her these targets the next time she asks me if I know how to use a gun.*

At the house LC checked her email and found a report in her inbox from the private investigator she'd hired.

Once he told her that Rita Simmons was the one following her, LC assigned him the job of following Rita.

Most of the pictures he sent were of Rita and her daughter, Donna. There were a couple of Rita and an unknown man.

LC studied the man's face. She didn't recognize him. She did recognize the look of hatred on his face when he looked at Rita. The most upsetting thing in the report was Rita paid regular visits to the condo building just north of LC's home.

What's that bitch up to? It's just too much of a coincidence that she spends so much time in that building.

CHAPTER 36

Amber was coming down the hallway headed to Supervising Agent Goldman's office. Voices coming from around the corner stopped her.

"Special Agent Hazelton, how is the investigation into Operation Surfs Up progressing?"

"So far so good. Seems like a case of self-defense; however, we still have a few things to check out. And we have a final interview scheduled with Detective Murdoch tomorrow morning at ten."

"Hmmm. Yes, well see to it that you're thorough. No need to rush to judgement."

Even though she couldn't see his face, Amber could hear that smug smile of his in his voice as he continued, "We wouldn't want to miss anything and acquit too hastily."

Hazelton's response was hesitant, and he sounded slightly confused. "No sir, we wouldn't want to do that."

"What about the other individual. That Carpenter woman, how's that moving along?"

"Yes sir, the problem is that the Bates case is a closed case that we don't have any jurisdiction over, so it's been a bit difficult getting more than just the basic information."

Goldman's tone turned hard. "Find a way to give us jurisdiction. Isn't she connected to the trafficking case Hoffner's working on?"

"Yes sir, she's the one who found Natalie Kramer's body and since..."

Amber heard the slap on the back, as Goldman said, "Well then, there's your connection. As a person involved in one of our cases, we have the right, no, the duty to investigate that person."

"Yes, sir." Hazelton's voice was firm but to Amber's ear there was something about his answer that didn't ring true. He paused, then, "What do I tell Special Agent Hoffner about me investigating Carpenter?"

"Special Agent Hoffner will simply have to learn that there are times when her job will conflict with outside friendships."

Amber had heard more than enough. She backed up several steps to the nearest cross corridor. Then whistling, she headed back to where she had overheard the conversation. When she rounded the corner, Hazelton was still standing in the corridor, watching Supervising Agent Goldman heading into his office. When he heard her, he turned around.

Looking directly into the man's eyes, she said, "Good morning, Special Agent Hazelton."

"Good..." he cleared his throat. "Good morning, Special Agent Hoffner."

"How goes the Incident Investigation?" Amber was doing her best to make casual conversation, to say things that she would normally say if she hadn't just heard what she had heard.

He straightened his tie. "You know I can't talk to you about the investigation."

She smiled. "Can't blame a girl for trying. See you around."

Forgetting all about where she had been going, Amber left the building, and started the drive to Coventry Beach. It was nearly an hour away and she hoped that My Place would still be open when she got there. She considered calling ahead and asking Harriet to stay open and to keep Murdoch there, until she arrived.

Paranoia got the better of her and she decided to skip the call. She knew where Murdoch lived. If she had to, she'd go to her home.

No sense in involving Harriet.

CHAPTER 37

Where the hell is Murdoch? My Place is closed. She's not home. I know she's not at LC's. Or is she?

She headed down the road to LC's beach house, but Murdoch's car wasn't in the driveway. Amber continued north looking for a place to get a cup of coffee while she tried to figure out where Murdoch could be. Driving past an off-beach parking lot she spotted Murdoch's car.

Having missed the entrance to the lot, she found a place to make a U-turn and doubled back. She parked next to Murdoch's car and got out.

At first it felt like stepping into a sauna. Then the sea breeze touched her and dried the slight perspiration that had instantly erupted. Still dressed in her FBI uniform, dark blue pant suit, white blouse, and black flats, Amber realized she probably should have taken time to change clothes.

Hardly beach attire.

An elderly man was sitting on a park bench, watching the ocean. "Excuse me, sir."

"Yes?"

She pointed at Murdoch's car. "Did you see where the woman from that car went?"

He looked at her suspiciously.

Amber flashed her FBI ID. "I need to speak with her, can you tell me where she is?"

His suspicious look turned into a smile. "Detective Murdoch is on the beach. Last I saw of her she was running south." He shook his head. "That woman loves to run in the soft sand."

"How long ago?"

He squinted at the ocean and glanced over his shoulder to the west. "'Bout a half-hour."

"Thank you." Amber got back in her car and headed south, to LC's house.

Standing at the front door leaning on the doorbell, Amber yelled. "I know you're in there. It's important. I need to talk to you."

Nothing. Then she heard the metallic click of the deadbolt being unlocked.

Amber opened the door and remembering that Tut was a flight risk, she stepped inside and closed the door behind her. At first, she didn't see LC, then she realized that she was out back on the lanai.

As she stepped onto the patio she asked, "Have you seen Murdoch?" Amber didn't notice the white noise app running on LC's phone.

"That's your idea of important. Get out."

Amber sighed. "Can we go for a walk?"

LC laughed. "You're not exactly dressed for a walk on the beach."

Amber was already removing her shoes, socks, and rolling up her pants legs. She tossed her jacket on a chair. "Let's go."

LC was still pissed at Amber but there was something about her manner, that caused LC to agree to go for a walk.

Part way down the path to the beach, LC turned off the white noise app. Neither woman said anything until they were walking on the hardpack with the waves rolling over their feet.

Amber quickly related the conversation she had overheard between Goldman and Hazelton. "Now you see why it's important that I find Murdoch."

"I don't get it. It sounds to me like your boss just wants a thorough investigation of the shooting."

"It wasn't so much the actual words as his tone. This guy, honestly, I don't know how he ever passed the psychological tests to be an agent."

LC's expression was confused.

"All agents have to pass certain psychological tests. It weeds out the Wyatt Earp types and the ones with prejudices toward women and minorities." Amber smiled. "We live in a very litigious society and the FBI hates getting bad press because some agent did something stupid."

"Whatever. I don't understand why he's interested in investigating me." She shrugged. "I'm not an agent. I simply had the misfortune of coming upon Natalie Kramer's body."

"Yeah, that's something else that Murdoch might be able to help me with. Did you see her earlier? The guy at the park said she left there about a half-hour, more like forty minutes ago now."

"She ran past moving south a while ago."

"You haven't seen her come back?"

"No, if she stays true to her routine, she'll be back by any minute now." LC looked down the beach and saw a figure running toward them. "That's probably her now."

LC and Amber moved inland toward the soft sand to intercept Murdoch.

"What are you two doing here?"

LC let her eyes feast on a sweaty out of breath Murdoch while Amber explained the situation. Usually when she saw Murdoch, the woman was fully clothed, long pants, polo shirt, and shoes. Now she was wearing running shorts, a sports bra, and no shoes. Her body heat made whatever it was she wore as a perfume waft off her in waves.

Instead of the usual aroma LC got from Murdoch, today she smelled like the cinnamon buns that Harriet made.

When Amber finished explaining the situation, Murdoch tilted her head back, and took several deep breaths. Then she looked Amber in the eyes and asked, "Why?"

Amber looked at her with a confused expression. Murdoch repeated her question. "Why? What does Goldman get out of screwing up my life and LC's life?"

Amber shook her head. "I don't get it. I mean if it were just a thing about women in law enforcement, but LC's not a cop." She paused. "Let me do some investigating." She smiled. "It'll give me a chance to reactivate my computer skills."

"I have an interview with the Incident Team tomorrow at 10:00 a.m. It'll be interesting to see what they have to say."

LC looked at Murdoch and said, "I'll get you the best criminal defense attorney in the state. If his schedule is free, he'll go to that interview with you."

The faintest of smiles touched Murdoch's lips. "Thank you but no. I want them to keep thinking that they have all the marbles." She looked from LC to Amber and back. "But I think

136

you should contact a lawyer yourself, put him on retainer. Remember Goldman's after you too."

LC smiled. "Thanks to you I already have an attorney on retainer. I'll call him and bring him up to speed."

CHAPTER 38

Murdoch checked in at the reception desk of the FBI Offices on the east side of Center City. "Detective Angela Murdoch, Hamilton County Sheriff's Office. I'm here for my 10:00 a.m. appointment with Special Agent Hazelton."

The young man behind the desk looked down at the papers on his desk. Then brought his eyes back up to meet Murdoch's. "I'll let Special Agent Hazelton know you're here."

Murdoch nodded and moved away from the desk. Standing at the large window looking out on the sunny street, Murdoch was thinking about how things had changed since her last visit to Special Agent Hazelton.

That time the receptionist gave her a Visitor Pass and sent her to the second floor, where Hazelton met her at the elevator.

This isn't going to be a pleasant visit. That much I can tell. Be interesting to see what happens.

Behind her she heard the quiet swish of elevator doors opening. Special Agent Hazelton stepped out, stopped at the desk, was handed a lanyard with a badge on it, and walked to where Murdoch was standing.

"Good morning, Detective Murdoch." He handed her the badge. "If you'll follow me."

"Good morning, Special Agent Hazelton. Lead the way." She put the lanyard on and noted that the badge wasn't the A level badge she had received the last time she was here.

Different levels of visitor badge determined your level of access and freedom of movement. Her current badge meant that she wasn't to move anywhere within the building without an agent to escort her.

Side-by-side they walked to the elevator. Hazelton pressed the button. The doors swished open, and Hazelton used the file folder in his hand to motion for Murdoch to precede him into the small cage.

While Murdoch wasn't exactly claustrophobic; she neither liked nor trusted elevators. She much preferred to use the stairs.

As she stepped out of the elevator Murdoch started to move to her right, but Hazelton said, "This way, please," as he indicated the hallway to the left, again using the file folder.

Murdoch hesitated and met his eyes. The camaraderie and respect she had seen there at their last meeting had been replaced by something else - suspicion.

"Sure." She followed him down the corridor, knowing that his office was in the opposite direction.

A few doors down Hazelton opened a door and ushered Murdoch into an interrogation room.

Murdoch schooled her face into an expressionless mask, reminding herself that her best course of action was to say nothing.

Hazleton offered Murdoch a seat and then moved to the one across the table from her. He dropped the file folder on the table, unbuttoned his jacket, and sat down.

Looking her in the eyes, he said, "You are aware this interview is being video recorded."

"Yes."

"You know your rights. Do you wish to have an attorney present for this interview?"

"Not at this time."

"Did you know the man you shot during Operation Surfs Up?"

"No."

Hazelton opened the folder. "His name was Lawrence Philpot. Most people called him Larry P or Jughead. Ring any bells."

"No."

Hazelton sat back in his chair and placed his right ankle on his left thigh and steepled his hands. "Sure about that?"

"Yes. Positive." Murdoch sat with an erect posture, her hands palm down on her legs, and her feet flat on the floor.

"Really." Hazelton put his foot back on the floor and leaned forward. He pushed a couple of pages from the folder across the table toward Murdoch. "Then how do you explain these text messages between you and the man you killed that night?"

Without touching the pages Murdoch leaned forward enough to read the printouts.

Hazelton watched her looking at the pages. "These were taken from Lawrence Philpot's phone. That is your number, isn't it?"

"Yes." *How the hell did they manage to create this evidence? What's Goldman's motive?*

"But you claim you don't know the sender, Lawrence Philpot?"

Murdoch sat back in her chair. "I don't know Lawrence Philpot and to the best of my knowledge have never received a text message from or responded to a text message from a Lawrence Philpot." She paused. "I think I'll avail myself of that attorney now."

CHAPTER 39

Amber was at My Place waiting for Murdoch to arrive. It was 12:30 p.m. and Murdoch's FBI interview was at 10:00 a.m. For the seventh time in five minutes, she looked up at the clock on the wall behind the counter.

Harriet was in the kitchen taking her frustration out on the dough for the fresh bread on the menu.

Amber stood up to go get a refill on her coffee when Murdoch opened the door. She paused just inside the café.

Harriet stood in the doorway to the kitchen. She looked from Murdoch to Amber and then back to Murdoch.

"Hey chère. What can I get for you today?"

Murdoch smiled. Harriet always seemed to have that effect on her. "Your company, coffee and an order of Beignets."

"I was headed for a refill anyway, so I'll get her coffee, Harriet." Amber said, as she moved toward the coffee pots behind the front counter.

Harriet nodded and headed back into the kitchen. By the time she reappeared with a plate of Beignets, Amber and Murdoch were seated. She placed the plate on the table, pulled a chair over, and said, "I can't visit long but I want to know what's going on."

Murdoch studied her coffee for a moment, then lifted her head and repositioned herself so she could see both women. "It seems the FBI thinks I killed Lawrence Philpot because he could implicate me in the human trafficking."

Harriet looked from Murdoch to Amber. "Somebody at the FBI is crazy."

Amber looked from Harriet to Murdoch. "I agree. What kind of evidence do they have?"

The right side of Murdoch's mouth moved up into an almost smile. "Someone has manufactured text messages sent to me from this Philpot character."

Her mind racing ninety miles a minute, Amber ran through a multitude of possibilities surrounding the purpose of such evidence being planted. In thirty seconds, she reached a decision.

She pulled a notepad out, wrote, "Keep talking" tore the page from the pad, and pushed it to the middle of the table. Then she turned her attention back to her notepad.

Murdoch and Harriet looked at each other and shrugged.

"Since it doesn't look like you're headed back to being a detective anytime soon, I could use your help around here."

Murdoch sighed. "Sure. Why not. All the coffee I can drink, Beignets, and donuts to eat. What more could a woman ask for?"

Harriet laughed. "I'll be paying you in more than coffee and donuts." She paused. "You can start tomorrow. Today's a slow day as a general rule."

Amber quickly scanned what she'd written, placed her cell phone on the table, and held the note pad up so both Harriet and Murdoch could read her note.

"Harriet, can I borrow your truck? Murdoch leave cell phone here. Harriet 911 number is, 3869227584. Will be back before closing time."

Harriet nodded, and scribbled the phone number on a napkin that she put in her apron.

Murdoch placed her cell phone on the table.

The three friends stood up. Harriet picked up the cell phones, dropped them in her apron pocket, and they all headed for the kitchen.

"Look, Murdoch don't worry about it. Goldman's too stupid to know how to manufacture that kind of evidence. It means he had help and the more people involved in a frame the weaker the frame."

"That's right, chère. Men are ruled by their little brain."

The women laughed.

In the kitchen, Harriet had her music on. She turned up the volume. The three women huddled close together.

Harriet handed Amber the keys to her 1988 F-150. "You two do what you have to do. I'll be here."

There were quick hugs all around and Amber and Murdoch, slipped out the back door of the kitchen. Murdoch started to say something as they climbed into the truck, but Amber silenced her with a shake of her head.

When they were a block away from the café, Amber said, "Now we can talk."

"All right. Explain why we're doing all the cloak and dagger."

"Sure. Harriet's truck is old enough that it doesn't have any built-in electronic tracking. I have a throw away phone I bought a long time ago and since we don't have our cell

144

phones with us, they can't be used to track us or to listen in on our conversation."

"What makes you think someone is tracking us?"

"Check your pockets." Murdoch looked at her, as if she were crazy. "Just humor me."

Murdoch released her seat belt to make it easier to get into her pockets. In her right back pocket, she found a small disc. "What the…?"

Holding it by the edges between her index finger and thumb, she held it up for Amber to see.

Amber smiled and popped a piece of gum into her mouth. "Hang onto it." She drove across the river to the mainland and into a shopping center parking lot.

Parked next to a newer version of Harriet's truck, she said, "Give me that thing." She took the tracking device and put her chewing gum on the bottom of it. Then she got out, leaned into the bed of the other truck, and placed the device in the back corner of the bed. She pushed it down so the gum would hold it in place, rather than have it rattling around in the truck bed.

CHAPTER 40

Amber drove back across the river, through several residential areas along the river, and finally came out north of LC's house on Atlantic Ocean Avenue. She continued north for a few miles and then turned west onto a two-lane road.

"It's been a long time since I've been here. There's a dirt road off to the right that I want to take. Keep your eyes open."

Moments later, Amber made an abrupt turn off the road. The dirt road, if you could call it a road, wound its way back to a clearing in the woods.

In the center of the clearing was a fire pit. Amber circled the firepit on the outer edges of the soft sand. The ground was firmer at the edge, with less risk of getting stuck in the sand. When the truck was positioned for the drive out, she turned off the engine.

The silence was amazing. The truck engine had disturbed the ecosystem and even the insects were silent. Not a leaf rustled, not a bird sang, as all the creatures waited to see what this new beast was going to do.

During the ride Murdoch was lost in thought. Amber's request for help in finding her turn off broke her reverie and now she looked around at where they were parked.

Tall slash pine trees, live oaks, palmettos, and various other trees and plants Murdoch didn't know the names of made up the surrounding woods. The aroma of burnt wood, citrus blossoms, and sea air mingled together. Now the buzz of insects and the songs of the local birds began to fill the air. Still, there were no manmade noises until Murdoch spoke.

"What is this place?"

Amber climbed out of the truck as she said, "Brian and I stumbled upon it during my last visit." She chuckled. "That boy loves to wander around in the woods. He's probably loving life in Idaho."

Murdoch got out of the truck and surveyed the area. There was the road they'd come in on and then there were two footpaths that led off in different directions. Both footpaths curved in opposite directions about twenty feet in, leaving the observer to wonder where they led.

Amber shook her head as if to erase her thoughts regarding Special Agent Brian Scott. "Anyway, we need to figure out what the end game is. Why is Goldman after you and LC?"

Murdoch took a deep breath and sighed. "Our connection is simple, she found Natalie Kramer's body and she witnessed a murder on the beach. Beyond that..."

"Are you really that blind?" Amber slammed the truck door behind her.

Murdoch got out of the truck and walked around to where Amber stood staring at the firepit. "What are talking about?"

Amber laughed. "For God's sake the woman is crazy about you and I'm pretty damn sure the feeling is mutual."

Murdoch turned her back on Amber and wandered to the trailhead closest to her. "You've been out in the Florida sun too long."

Amber crossed her arms, tilted her head to the right, and with a smile on her face said, "Really? Then you look me in the eyes and deny that you have feelings for Larissa Carpenter."

Murdoch drew a long, deep breath, straightened her shoulders, and turned to face Amber. "Don't we have more important things to talk about than my supposed feelings for LC?"

"No! Because I think those mutual feelings are behind this whole situation."

Murdoch sighed. "I think you read too many romance novels."

Amber smiled. "Actually, I don't read romance novels. I read technology manuals, programming books, and…"

"Whatever!" Murdoch advanced on Amber. Standing close enough to be in Amber's personal space, "I don't give a rodent's rosy, red rectum what you read. What makes you think that some imaginary feelings between LC and me are behind all of this?"

With a partial smile on her face, both hands palms up, Amber raised her shoulders. "I don't know why I think it." She relaxed her shoulders and dropped her hands. "There's just something… Face it the only connection between you and LC is that she's reported various crimes. Two murders that aren't connected and you killed a woman in the process of saving her life."

Murdoch backed off a step and ran her hands through her short hair, leaving it standing on end on top of her head. She turned away from Amber and surveyed the surroundings. Then brought her attention back to Amber. "Why are we here? I mean, why specifically this location. We could have gone for a walk on the beach. Why here?"

"The agents following you know you go to the beach. They're probably visiting all of your regular haunts to try and pick up your trail, assuming they know we ditched the tracking device Hazelton planted on you." Smiling, she tilted her head back and closed her eyes. "You've never been here before and I doubt they know about this place. Regardless, they know I'm with you and if Hazelton's as smart as he should be, he'll be reaching out to Brian soon. And he might just remember this place, so let's get down to brass tacks."

Murdoch reviewed the evidence that Hazelton showed her that morning. "The text messages were vague. It's not what they said but simply the fact that this joker was texting me and I was responding."

"Yeah. Larry Philpot's phone is in the evidence locker at the FBI, along with a million other things." Amber paced back and forth. "All anyone would need to do is find out Philpot's phone number, with that creating the text trail is easy. The hard part is making it sound like him and make the response sound like you. Did the replies sound like the way you text?"

"What do you mean?"

"Did the way the replies were worded sound like you? We all have our own way of talking and texting. Did they sound like you?"

Murdoch paced between the two trailheads. "I'm not sure. I didn't pay that close attention. I mean, come on, I knew they were going to pull something but..."

"I get it. Had to be a shock to find out you'd been texting with the guy you shot. Let me think." Amber silently stared off into the distance, occasionally tilting her head one way then the other. Just as Murdoch was about to say something, Amber said, "While it would be risky to take the phone out of the evidence locker, it would be easy enough to go in with another phone and create a clone."

"You know how to do that?"

"Yes, unfortunately a lot of people know how to do it and with a little instruction, a few uninterrupted minutes with the real phone, the right software, and making a *complete* clone would be child's play." She paused and looked at Murdoch. "Even Goldman could manage it."

"What's the difference between a complete clone and a clone?"

"A complete clone not only steals your phone's identity, it also copies all the data on the phone. Address book, text threads, you name it. Basically, it's a duplicate of the target phone." She shrugged. "With a complete clone, writing texts that sound like the owner of the target phone would be easy because you have their old text messages to look at." She sighed. "That leaves them with the challenge of making the replies sound like you."

"Sounds like a lot of effort. But just for arguments sake, let's say that you're right. That's how it was done. Why? Why go to all that trouble to frame me?"

Amber silently stared off into the distance, occasionally tilting her head one way then the other. Just as Murdoch was about to say something, Amber looked at her and said, "Follow the money."

Murdoch snorted. "What money? I have maybe five thousand dollars in savings."

"Yes, but Larissa has lots of money."

Murdoch sighed. "Yes but…"

"While neither of you is willing to admit to the other that you care about each other. Other people can see it, and someone is planning on taking advantage of those feelings."

CHAPTER 41

Rita Simmons sat in her car on the driveway admiring the beach house. *I could take this place as part of the settlement.* She sighed. *But I think not. I want to get out of this state. Maybe the mountains. Definitely some place that has seasons. I'm sick of being hot all the time.*

Knowing Larissa's routine, Rita knew that she would most likely be out back on the lanai, so she took the path around to the back of the house.

Larissa heard the slap of Rita's sandals on the pavers long before she saw her. Having only met Rita once, several years ago, she didn't recognize her.

"Whatever you're selling, I'm not buying. Please, leave."

Rita smiled. "Believe me, what I'm selling is something you're definitely going to want to buy." She paused. "Unless of course, you don't care if Detective Angela Murdoch ends up in jail."

Larissa stood up, slipped Tut into the house, closed the sliding glass door, and moved toward the woman standing at the door.

"What are you babbling about? Who are you?"

Rita emitted a small laugh. She removed the large straw hat and oversized sunglasses. "I suppose I shouldn't be surprised that you don't remember me. We did only meet the one time."

"Rita Simmons. Yes, I remember the evening you disowned Rachel. What do you want?"

"Half. Half of everything." The confused look on Larissa's face was amusing to Rita.

"What makes you think I'll give you more than a swift kick in the ass?"

Rita stepped closer to the door. "Because if you don't give me half of everything. The text messages between Larry Philpot and Detective Angela Murdoch, will put the detective in jail, or at the very least ruin her career and her reputation."

Amber had phoned earlier to tell Larissa that she and Murdoch were on their way to see her. Some of the pieces of the problems Murdoch was having were falling into place. She wanted Rita to still be there when the others arrived. She had to stall.

"Start at the beginning and explain to me exactly what you think you have that I'm going to pay for."

"God are you really that thick?" Since she always had a less than stellar opinion of Larissa, it was easy for her to believe that she simply didn't understand the situation. Rita was more than happy to explain her brilliant plan.

"I'm not going to stand out here in the heat. Invite me inside and we'll talk."

Larissa opened the door and motioned Rita in. Then she repeated the operation with the slider.

Though she loathed to be civil to this woman she said, "Would you like some tea or coffee?"

"No. I didn't come here to socialize. I came here to tell you why you're going to give me half of everything you have." She looked around the beach house. Nothing about it appealed to her. "You can keep this place. If you can still afford it after I'm through with you."

Larissa poured herself a cup of coffee and indicated a stool at the bar for her guest. Instead, Rita chose the chair at the breakfast table where her back was to a wall.

Looking at Rita over her coffee cup, Larissa said, "I'm listening."

Rita smiled. "I'll use little words so as not to confuse you. I have a person in position with enough evidence of your beloved Murdoch's involvement with the recent human trafficking ring to put her behind bars. Even if she manages to avoid doing time, her reputation and career will be ruined."

"I see."

"Once you've transferred $552,345,000.00 to my account, I'll provide that person with the proof that the information was manufactured in an effort to discredit Murdoch." She shrugged. "After all, Larry Philpot was Mr. Smith's illegitimate child. It's only natural he would want revenge on the person that killed the boy."

Larissa sipped her coffee. "How do I know that you won't just take the money and disappear with the evidence to save Murdoch?"

"I guess you'll just have to trust me."

Larissa's computer that was on the breakfast bar notified her that a car was in the driveway. She looked at the screen. It was Amber and Murdoch.

Rita stood up. "You have twenty-four hours. I'll be back tomorrow with the account information."

"Fine." Larissa led the way to the front door. She opened it just as Amber, and Murdoch arrived at it. She looked at Rita. "We'll conclude our business then."

Rita smiled and nodded her head in agreement. "Until tomorrow." She nodded at Amber and Murdoch. "Ladies."

Murdoch and Amber watched Rita get in her car. "If Tut escapes while you two stand there gawking, you get to chase him down."

They followed Larissa into the house as they looked around for the cat. He was in his favorite chair, grooming himself.

"Who was that?" Amber asked.

"No one." Larissa pulled her phone out and turned on the white noise app. "Exactly why are you two here again?"

Murdoch and Amber exchanged glances. Before Murdoch could speak Amber jumped in. "Was that no one here to blackmail you into paying her to make the evidence against Murdoch disappear?"

Murdoch was about to object to Amber's hypothetical when she saw the look on Larissa's face. Unable to find words, she looked at Amber. "How did…?"

"She's Rachel's Aunt Rita, isn't she?"

All Larissa could do was nod her head.

"I have a friend in Central City send me a copy of the whole incident involving Rachel's death, including the irate relatives who expected to get rich out of her passing. Rita was the ringleader".

Murdoch lowered herself to a bar stool. "I don't believe it. What could she possibly expect to gain by framing me?"

Amber sighed. "I already explained all of that to you."

Shaking her head in disbelief, Murdoch said, "But she can't really expect LC to pay her." Looking from Larissa to Amber and back, Murdoch stood up. "I refuse to let you pay her extortion. I'll…"

Having recovered from her initial shock that Amber had figured everything out, Larissa felt an instant flush of rage. Her jaw muscles jumping, eyes narrowed, in a quiet voice she said, "Get out. Both of you."

"But…"

"But nothing. My money. My decision. You know where the door is." Without waiting for a reply Larissa headed for the beach.

CHAPTER 42

Neither woman spoke during the short drive to My Place. When Amber parked behind the café, they sat in the truck for a moment, staring straight ahead. Then they both started to speak at once.

"I don't want…"

"Look we really…"

They both laughed, followed by a momentary silence, which Amber broke. "Look, we need to concentrate on figuring out which one of the local slimeballs Rita used to create those text messages." Murdoch started to say something, but Amber cut her off. "Yes, I know Goldman had to be the one who cloned the phone. However, I don't think he's stupid enough to actually hire someone to manufacture evidence. Most likely, he gave the phone to Rita, and she took it from there."

"Yeah, whatever, I just don't want LC paying her any kind of extortion on my behalf. Not that I really think she would." She looked at Amber. "Would she? I mean, really, why? It's not like we're a couple or even friends."

Shaking her head and sighing Amber said, "I already gave you my opinion on the situation."

Murdoch laughed. "I never realized what a romantic you are." She got out of the truck and headed for the kitchen door. "I'll reach out to some of my sources and see if I can figure out who was hired. There aren't a lot of high-tech criminals in Coventry Beach. Most likely whoever it was is in Central City." She paused at the door and turned to face Amber, who was right behind her. "Let's not worry Harriet with any of this. You and I just went someplace quiet to talk about my situation. No need to mention anything about LC."

Amber nodded. "Agreed."

The door was unlocked, and the two women stepped into the kitchen. Harriet was sitting in her office preparing her bank deposit. The two law enforcement officers looked at each other in disbelief.

"Harriet, do you realize how dangerous it is for you to leave the back door unlocked, especially when you've got all that money laying around in plain sight?"

Smiling, Harriet looked at the two women. "I heard my old truck pull up. I knew it was you two" she turned and pushed a key combination on her computer and the deadbolt slid into place "so I unlocked the door. You were probably still in the truck and just didn't hear it."

The sound of the deadbolt moving into place, caused both women to look at the door. "Larissa suggested the setup and it really wasn't all that expensive."

Harriet took the money from her desk and placed it in the deposit bag. "So, what have you two ladies been doing?" She stood up from her desk and proffered each of her visitors their cell phones.

Murdoch jumped in with, "Just talking about how to discredit these text messages supposedly sent to and from me. And with that end in mind, I'm going to take off I have some people to contact. I'll see you tomorrow for breakfast."

Before Amber could respond her phone notified her of a text message. She glanced at the device. The message was from LC.

We need to talk. No Murdoch.

"I'll walk out with you. I have to check in with work too." Amber turned to Harriet. "You going to be all right to lock up and get to the bank by yourself?"

Harriet laughed as she walked the two women to the front door. "Yes, I do it every day without an escort. You two go figure out who's behind this nonsense?"

Locking the door behind her two friends, Harriet wondered how Larissa fit into all of this.

CHAPTER 43

Amber pulled into LC's driveway. Almost immediately the garage door went up and she pulled in next to LC's car. As soon as she turned off the engine the door went down.

She knocked on the door to the house.

"Come on in, Amber."

Standing on the table near the door, Tut greeted her. She reached out and rubbed the cat's head. He pushed on her hand, purring.

"Thanks for coming back."

Amber looked at her friend. Her face was an expressionless mask, but the tenseness of her body gave away the fact that she was upset.

"That's what friends do. How can I help?"

Larissa smiled, slightly. "I thought you'd never ask. Can I get you anything? Coffee? Tea? A snack?"

"No thanks."

"Okay." She led the way to the patio. Once they were seated, she began, "First off, I don't want Murdoch to know I'm paying Rita off." Amber started to speak but Larissa cut her off. "I don't want her to feel like she owes me anything. It's my money and my choice." She sighed. "I don't give a damn about the money. I just don't like the idea of Rita getting away with this little stunt. So how can we make her pay for this? Preferably without Murdoch ever finding out I had anything to do with it."

"How and when is the payoff supposed to happen?" Amber could tell it was an effort for LC to maintain a calm exterior.

"She's coming to see me tomorrow, the same time she was here today. I have a feeling she'll be here earlier though. To catch me off guard, unprepared." She took a deep breath. "I'm having sufficient funds moved to a specific account from which I will transfer the money she's demanding."

Amber hesitated, then asked, "Just how much is she demanding, if you don't mind me asking?"

LC laughed. "In other words, how much is Murdoch worth to me?"

"Never mind. It's none of my business."

"$552,345,000.00."

Under other circumstances LC would have been amused by the look on Amber's face.

"Wow!"

"Yeah, wow. I don't care about the money. I do care about clearing Murdoch's name. According to the bitch, after I transfer the money, she'll provide evidence to the FBI that the text messages were faked."

"You trust her to do that?"

"Hell no! That's why I want you to track the money as it leaves my account." LC passed a small piece of paper to Amber. "That's my account number. I want you to put a listening device in the breakfast area. Rita's not going to want to sit outside. She's far too delicate a flower for the Florida heat and humidity."

Amber's eyebrows went up. "Don't you already have a listening device in your house?" She pointed at LC's phone that was running the white noise app. "Isn't that why you're running that app?"

"The problem is I don't know whose device it is. However, considering recent events, I believe it belongs to Rita." She paused. "And when the time is right, I plan on giving it back to her."

LC stood up indicating the meeting was over. "I'll get her to read me the account number. After I enter it, I'll read it back to her, to make sure I got it right." She smiled. "I mean, I wouldn't want to accidentally transfer all that money to someone else's account. Can you follow the money electronically?"

"Yes, especially since I have your account number to start with. Once it reaches its destination what do you want me to do?"

"Just monitor it. If she transfers it out of that account I want to know where she sends it."

"What will you do if she doesn't clear Murdoch?"

LC smiled. "When can you get the listening device set up?"

CHAPTER 44

Murdoch entered Martins Pub, and let her eyes adjust to the dim lighting as she looked around.

Martins was a quiet neighborhood pub and grill. The front area was L shaped. In front of her to the right was the longest part of the L shaped bar, between that section of the bar and the front window were a few tables. Directly in front of her was the main dining / drinking area. The entrance to the kitchen was on the wall just past the short end of the L shaped bar. On that same wall, just past the kitchen entrance was a table.

As she had suspected Donald Cook was at that table.

"Hello Donald."

The fork full of Shepherd's Pie finished the journey to his mouth and he motioned for Murdoch to have a seat.

A waitress happened by while Donald was finishing his bite. "Murdoch, we haven't seen you in here in a while."

"Yeah, life gets in the way of fun all too often."

"What can I get you?"

"Root beer, no ice."

"Coming up."

Murdoch turned her attention back to Donald, who was washing his Shepherd's Pie down with a swallow of beer. "What can I do for you, Detective Murdoch?"

"I need a favor."

"Like I said, what can I do for you?"

"There are a couple of people I need information on. Rita Simmons and Michael P. Goldman." Something about Donald's face, caused Murdoch to pause. "You're already investigating at least one of them, aren't you?"

Donald smiled. "Now you know I can't tell you anything about a case I'm working on, at least not without a court order." He paused. "Do you have a court order?"

Murdoch leaned back in her chair. "No and even if I could get one, I don't have time for that." She laughed. "Maybe the favor you can do, is to hire me after this is all over. That's assuming I stay out of jail." The waitress delivered Murdoch's root beer. She started to put a straw on the table next to the glass. "Thanks, keep the straw."

Donald waited for the waitress to depart before speaking. "You know Murdoch, I'd be happy to have you on my staff, but I'd rather have a friend on the force." He paused, looking around the pub. The pool room beyond the half wall to his right was empty and the closest occupied table was on the far side of the room. He opened the briefcase on the chair between himself and Murdoch. "It's nice to get out of the office and do some paperwork in a different environment, once in a while." He smiled, took another sip of beer and said, "The problem I have is, this beer seems to go right through me. I'll be right back."

Murdoch watched Donald's reflection in the mirror on the pool room wall as he turned down the hall for the bathrooms. As soon as he was out of sight, she pulled the chair holding the briefcase around where she had easier access to the files she could see.

The second file folder down was her target. Carpenter, L.

Jackpot. She didn't waste time looking at the photos or the surveillance reports, instead she used her phone to photograph each picture and document. By the time Donald came back Murdoch was finishing her root beer.

CHAPTER 45

At home Murdoch printed out everything she'd photographed from Donald Cook's file.

As the last item was coming off the printer someone knocked on her door. A moment of panic gripped her, and she thought, "This is what they feel like when I knock on their door and they're about to get busted. Can't say I like being on this side of the door."

"Who is it?" On her way to the door, she dropped the stack of papers on the coffee table in the living room.

"Pizza delivery," answered an amused voice.

Murdoch recognized Amber's voice.

"You better actually have a pizza." Murdoch opened the door and was met with the delicious smell of hot cheese and pepperoni. In addition, Amber was carrying a chilled six pack of Murdoch's favorite root beer.

With slices of pizza on paper plates, paper towels for napkins, and bottles of root beer wrapped in zip up cozies from Murdoch's favorite seafood restaurant, the two women sat down on the couch in the living room.

Amber immediately noticed the stack of papers on the coffee table. "What's all this?" She put her plate down and picked up the papers. Leafing through them, she asked, "Where did you get this?"

Answering around a mouthful of pizza, Murdoch said, "Let's just say I found it."

Looking from the papers to Murdoch and back, Amber replied, "Some find." She moved her plate off the table, put it next to her on the couch, and spread the papers out in chronological order, matching photos to reports.

"It looks like LC hired this PI to find out who was following her. Rita Simmons. Not much of a surprise there. Then she had him follow Simmons."

Taking a bite of pizza as she scanned the written reports, Amber asked, "Why didn't she tell us about any of this?"

Murdoch stopped chewing, swallowed and replied, "Really? You have to ask that question? Put yourself in her place. Would you trust us?"

Laughing Amber said, "I suppose not." She continued pushing the papers around and then stopped and stared at the photo she was holding. "Well, I'll be damned." She held the photo up for Murdoch to see. "Do you know who that is?"

Murdoch studied it for a moment. "No, but obviously you do."

"Damn right I do. That is FBI Supervising Agent Michael P. Goldman."

Murdoch took the picture, pointing at Goldman's hand, "What's that? It looks like he's handing her something." She reached into the drawer of the end table and grabbed a magnifying glass. "It's a phone."

"So, you were right. He cloned Philpot's phone and gave it to Simmons." She paused and then began rifling through the pictures. "If there's a picture of her with Goldman, maybe there's a picture of her with whoever created the text messages."

Looking at a picture of a young woman at Rita Simmons front door, Murdoch asked, "This is later the same day as she got the phone. Does the report say who this is?"

Amber smiled, "Donna Simmons, daughter of Rita Simmons."

Murdoch jumped to her feet and began pacing the room, running her hands through her hair.

"What is it?"

Tilting her head back, looking at the ceiling Murdoch took a deep breath, and then brought her eyes back to Amber. Laughing she said, "Sometimes we women are as prejudiced against our own gender as men. We keep talking like we're looking for a man. What do you want to bet that Donna Simmons is the missing piece to the puzzle?"

Amber pulled out her phone and started texting.

Murdoch asked, "What are you doing?"

Never looking up from her phone, "Just checking on something."

Moments later Amber received a text message. "Seems you're right. Donna Simmons is quite the geek. She won multiple science fairs in high school. All her projects were computer related."

"How did you…? You texted LC?"

"Of course, I texted LC. It's not like she doesn't know what's going on." Shaking her head in disbelief Amber returned to the photos and documents. "Let's go over what we know and what we think we know."

Murdoch returned to pacing. "We know the text messages are fake. At least, I know it. We know that Goldman passed a phone to Rita Simmons. We know that Rita Simmons' daughter Donna is capable of creating the false text message trail."

"Yes, and Rita Simmons is blackmailing LC for a sizeable chunk of money."

Murdoch stopped pacing and looked at Amber. "We *know* this?"

Damn! She doesn't know the amount of the extortion demand.

"Well, we know she's blackmailing LC and it only makes sense that it be for a large amount or why bother." Amber held Murdoch's gaze.

"Sure, if you say so. Here's something we don't know – why is Goldman working with Rita Simmons?"

Amber leaned back on the sofa and watched Murdoch pace. After a few moments she sat up. "Maybe he's not working with her voluntarily. She could be blackmailing him."

"What do you know about him?"

Amber sighed. "Not much. He was in Chicago before here and he's only been here a week or two. He got here just before I came back from DC. I think he's married and has a kid or two."

Murdoch flopped onto the couch and took another bite of pizza.

Amber stood up. "Get some sleep. I've talked to Hazelton. He already has the cyber division confirming the authenticity of those text messages and examining Philpot's phone to see if it's been cloned. I'll see you tomorrow at Harriet's for breakfast."

CHAPTER 46

Amber's phone woke her at 5:00 a.m. She looked at the screen. *Hazelton.* She flopped back onto her pillow. *What the hell can he possibly want at this hour?*

"What can I do for you Special Agent Hazelton?"

"We've found something you'll want to see. How soon can you be here?"

Special Agent Hoffner pulled into the FBI parking lot behind Murdoch. They parked next to one another and met on the sidewalk in front of the cars.

"I take it you got a call from Special Agent Hazelton, too."

Amber laughed. "Yeah." She glanced from Murdoch to the imposing building. "I wonder what he found."

"Well, we're not going to find out standing in the parking lot."

"Yeah, I guess not."

The building was locked at this hour. Amber placed her left hand on the scanner, while her hand was scanned, she punched in the code for having a guest with her. They heard the door unlock.

In the elevator, Murdoch said, "I wonder how he thought I was going to get in the building if we hadn't arrived at the same time."

Amber smiled. "I'm sure you would have figured something out."

The elevator door opened. Murdoch followed Amber down the silent corridor to the Cyber Unit's lab.

Stepping inside the room a feeling of nostalgia washed over Amber. A room like this was where she started with the FBI.

The coolness of the room combined with the hum of electronics, soothed her nerves. Her fingers twitched as though they were longing for a keyboard. She shook off the feeling and reminded herself why she was there. Hazelton was across the room talking with a tech she recognized.

"Hey Willie, how goes it?"

The young woman with Hazelton turned and smiled when she saw her. "Hi Amber. How're you liking field work?"

"It has its moments."

"Willie this is Det. Angela Murdoch. Murdoch, Willie is the second-best cyber cop you'll ever meet."

"Nice to meet you, Willie." She extended her hand, Willie shook it, and seemed unwilling to let go of it.

"If you're the second-best, who's the best?" Murdoch's gaydar had started pinging as soon as she saw the blonde standing with Hazelton.

Amber was so busy watching the sparks between Murdoch and Willie, she forgot to say that she was the best cyber-cop.

Hazelton cleared his throat and said, "I think it's time we showed our guests what you've found."

Willie winked at Murdoch, released her hand, and turned to Hazelton. "Of course. The person who created the text messages that were supposedly sent between Lawrence Philpot and Det. Murdoch must have been in a real hurry.

172

They were sloppy and left a trail a blind man could follow." She paused and turned to her keyboard. She called up a video. "As for how they got Philpot's phone… This is a video of Supervising Agent Goldman entering the evidence locker. He signed in to review the evidence in Operation Surfs Up." She paused the video, leaving the image of Goldman's face on her computer screen. Willie turned from the monitor and staring directly at Murdoch said, "Why he would be helping someone frame you is something we have yet to discover." She smiled. "But we will."

Hazelton looked at Murdoch. "I have a plan to find out who Goldman is helping and why, but I'll need your help, Det. Murdoch."

"Of course."

CHAPTER 47

Amber looked from Hazelton to Murdoch and back to Hazelton. "I think I know who Goldman is working with or for. The answer I don't have is why."

Hazelton looked at her questioningly but didn't say a word.

Murdoch clenched her jaw. She too knew who Goldman was working with. *What makes a man with a stellar FBI career go bad? Why throw it all away?*

Amber sighed. "Rita Simmons is attempting to extort money from Larissa Carpenter. She's admitted to being the one who framed Murdoch and to clear her Larissa has to pay Simmons."

Hazelton asked, "Why would someone pay..." He looked at Murdoch and then back to Amber. Shaking his head, he continued, "Never mind. Willie, I want to…"

"Yes, I know find out everything I can about Rita Simmons, especially any connection to Goldman. On it."

Murdoch started to speak but the look she got from Amber silenced her.

"When and how is Carpenter supposed to pay off this Simmons?"

Amber took a deep breath and explained LC's plan to Hazelton.

"As long as Goldman doesn't know we're on to him, the plan to get Simmons should work." He held Amber's gaze. "As soon as the money is transferred, we'll bring Goldman in for questioning." He paused and turned to Murdoch. "Change of plans, detective, looks like I won't need your help after all."

A short time later Amber and Murdoch left FBI HQ. As they walked to their cars each was lost in her own thoughts. On the sidewalk in front of the cars, Murdoch stopped and started to speak but Amber spoke first.

"I know you don't like the idea of LC paying off Rita Simmons, but it's her money and she should be able to do whatever she wants with it."

Murdoch nodded her head. "I only have one question – how much?"

Amber hesitated. She was sure that LC didn't want Murdoch to know how much she was willing to pay to clear Murdoch's name but at the same time she felt that maybe if Murdoch knew she would realize how much LC cared for her.

"You're going to be tracking the money, so I know you know the amount. What is it?"

"Half." Amber took a deep breath. "Half of everything LC has, $552,345,000.00."

Murdoch swallowed hard. "I…I…What?"

Laughing, Amber said, "When this is all over the two of you need to have a serious conversation."

CHAPTER 48

Larissa had already been up for a few hours when Amber's text message came in. *On my way to you. ETA 20 minutes. Got it.*

As she approached the house Amber used the remote control for the garage that LC had given her the day before. LC didn't want Amber's government issue SUV in the driveway, where it would be visible to anyone passing by, as well as visible from the condos to the north.

As soon as she was inside the garage, she killed her engine and put the door down. The less time it was up, the less likely anyone would see her car.

She knocked on the door to the house, then opened it and entered. Tut jumped up on the table next to the door and greeted her.

"Hello, your majesty" she said, as she rubbed the cat's head.

From the lanai LC called, "Get yourself something to drink and join me."

Amber grabbed a cup of coffee and sat in the chair Tut usually occupied.

"Did you have any trouble getting the bug?"

"No. Hazelton woke up a judge this morning to get the legalities taken care of."

"Hazleton? Isn't he the one trying to bury Murdoch?"

"No, he's the one Goldman was trying to get to, as you put it, bury Murdoch. He found the text messages were bogus." She paused, studying LC. "Murdoch's been cleared. Though that's not public knowledge yet."

She took a sip of her coffee and looked at LC. "You won't actually need to transfer any money."

"Really?"

"Yes, really. The Cyber Unit proved the text messages were planted and we have video of the agent that cloned the phone that made it possible to plant the text messages. As soon as Rita Simmons is arrested that agent will be brought in for questioning."

"You're sure that we don't actually have to pay the money to get her convicted?"

"All you have to do is get her to demand the payment in exchange for clearing Murdoch of any wrongdoing."

LC smiled. "Getting Rita to be demanding has never been a problem."

CHAPTER 49

Amber was gone. The bug was installed. All that remained was to wait for Rita to arrive.

LC sat by herself on the lanai thinking about what she was going to do when this nonsense was finished.

"What do you think, Tut? Should we go away for a bit? Maybe we should spend the rest of the summer in the mountains." She grabbed her phone and began looking at places to buy or rent in the foothills of the Appalachians.

"Georgia or North Carolina?"

Tut looked up at her as if to say, "I really don't care."

"Oh well, plenty of time to decide." She put her phone down, her feet up, and closed her eyes. The quiet sounds of the shore soon lulled her to sleep.

The alarm on her phone went off an hour before Rita was expected. LC woke up, turned off the alarm, and stretched. Her motion disturbed Tut causing him to get up and move to his own chair.

"My apologies, your majesty, but I need to get ready to receive the wicked witch of the south."

At the kitchen sink she splashed some water on her face and looked around the house. Despite the fact that this was Rachel's dream house, nothing in it reminded her of Rachel.

Rachel hadn't been around when she furnished the place. She laughed. *Hell, I wasn't around when I furnished this place. I picked stuff out from a website and had the property management company deal with the delivery.*

She took a deep breath and let it out slowly. *I like it here. I think I just need some time away to clear my mind and make some decisions about what I'm going to do with the rest of my life.*

Her thoughts were interrupted by a notification that a car was in the driveway. LC took her laptop and sat at the breakfast nook table. Knowing that Rita would want to sit with her back to the wall, LC smiled as she took that chair.

She watched the monitor and saw that Rita hadn't come alone. Her daughter, Donna was with her. As the two women reached the door, LC used the security system to unlock the deadbolt, then she called out, "It's unlocked." That was as close to an invitation to come in as those two people were ever going to get from her.

The physical appearance between the two women was striking. There was no doubt that Rita was Donna's mother. From what little LC knew of Rachel's uncle, she wondered if he was Donna's father.

LC watched Rita take a visual survey of the area. Then rather than sit at the table she turned one of the bar stools around to face the table and sat with her back to the bar. Donna copied her mother's actions.

No one spoke for several moments. Finally, Rita asked, "Do you have my money ready to transfer?"

"Remind me why I'm transferring money to you."

179

Rita sighed. "Because if you don't the woman you love will lose her career in law enforcement and possibly end up doing time."

"How is paying you going to change that?"

"I can prove the evidence against her was planted. That she wasn't involved in the human trafficking ring and that it really was self-defense to kill Lawrence Philpot." A smirk turned her lips up into what resembled a smile. "I can even have the evidence released that proves you didn't kill Natalie Kramer."

LC processed that last statement. "I should have known that you had something to do with me still being a person of interest in that mess." She moved her hands to the keyboard. "Give me a minute."

"Certainly."

"Tell me the exact dollar amount, again."

"$552,345,000.00"

"Okay, what's the account number?"

Rita read the account number and then LC read it back to her. "I wouldn't want to send all that money to the wrong account."

"No, we wouldn't want that."

"Done."

Rita looked at her phone and saw an email come in from her bank, verifying a deposit. She didn't check the amount. "Excellent. It's been a pleasure doing business with you."

LC said nothing. She stood up and walked to the front door. Rita and Donna followed her. Before opening the door LC, pulled a small plastic bag from her pocket. She handed it to Rita. "I believe this belongs to you."

Rita recognized the listening device and smiling said, "Thank you. These are hard to come by."

LC smiled. "You're welcome."

She opened the door.

FBI Special Agent Amber Hoffner said, "Rita and Donna Simmons you need to come with us."

"Mother, you said…"

"Shut up!" She turned and glared at LC. "You'll regret this."

"I rather doubt that. You see the FBI isn't quite as incompetent as you thought. They already figured out that the text messages were planted. As for me, well I'm sure once they question your accomplice, they'll figure out I had nothing to do with Natalie Kramer's murder or with the trafficking ring."

As Amber's colleagues took the two women away, she looked at LC and asked, "Why did you transfer the money? I told you it wasn't necessary."

Still smiling LC said, "The $5,535.00 I transferred to her account means nothing to me and it will help ensure her conviction."

CHAPTER 50

Sitting on the lanai, a cup of coffee at hand, and Tut in my lap I felt relaxed for the first time since – since when? Since meeting Natalie Kramer? Or since tripping over her body on the beach?

I closed my eyes and pulled in a long, deep breath of sea air. Tut was purring and all was right with the world. Well, almost all.

The human trafficking ring was destroyed, though being a realist, I had little doubt that someone would come along and pick up where Mr. Smith and company left off. I had been cleared of any connection to Natalie Kramer's murder and of any connection to Mr. Smith's enterprises. Murdoch was also cleared of any wrongdoing in the death of Lawrence Philpot.

Murdoch. What is it about that woman that makes me so crazy?

On the table next to my chair, the screen of my laptop lit up. I glanced over to see that Murdoch had just pulled into the driveway.

With barely a moment's hesitation I closed the laptop, draped the cat around my neck, picked up my coffee, the laptop, and quietly slipped into the house. At the foot of the stairs, I paused. For a second, I thought about answering the front door. Instead, I went upstairs and waited for Murdoch to leave.

About The Author

A native Floridian, Darlene has moved away multiple times, only to be drawn back by the smell of the sea, the sun, and the feel of sand between her toes. She and her spouse live near Darlene's hometown of Daytona Beach.

At the time of this writing, they have one rescue cat named Keke. She's part Russian Blue and quite often Darlene believes the cat is channeling a dog. Keke loves to follow her around and sit on the floor near her chair while she writes.

OTHER BOOKS IN THIS SERIES

A New Beginning in Coventry Beach
A Larissa Carpenter Mystery #1

Larissa Carpenter is the one of the richest women in the country. Eighteen months ago, her spouse, Rachel, died of a brain aneurysm. Looking for a new beginning, she travels to the small town of Coventry Beach and moves into the house she and Rachel bought just before Rachel died.

Using the name Laurel Carpenito to avoid the notoriety that came with winning the largest lottery jackpot in the state's history, she begins to clear her head and think about the future.

Finding the body of a young woman she'd met only 12 hours earlier wasn't part of the future Larissa/Laurel envisioned. As if being a person of interest in one murder wasn't bad enough, she witnesses a woman stab a man on the beach in front of her house.

At the local tea and coffee shop, My Place, Laurel runs into an old high school classmate who, unknown to Larissa/Laurel, is now an FBI agent.

The owner of My Place, Harriet Walsh, has spent two years running from an ex-fiancé turned stalker. Thinking he's lost her trail, she has settled down in Coventry Beach. She and Laurel have become friends, and when Harriet disappears, Det. Murdoch is unhappy with Laurel's hiring of a search and rescue team to help find Harriet.

Will Larissa find a new beginning in Coventry Beach, or will this be just another dip in the roller-coaster ride that her life has become?

Fatal Misunderstanding
A Larissa Carpenter Mystery #3

Follow Larissa Carpenter and four friends on a pre-All Hallows Eve girls' weekend in the mystic town of Cerridwen. The fun comes to an end with the discovery of a dead witch in a cottage in the woods and suspicions about at least one of the women begins. It turns out that the dead woman is the former lover of Larissa Carpenter's current friend with benefits. After spending weeks avoiding Det. Angela Murdoch, Larissa is forced to call her.

"Ms. Carpenter, you report more dead bodies to me than the 911 dispatcher," said Det. Angela Murdoch.

OTHER BOOKS BY THIS AUTHOR

The Legend of Erin Foster

Available as Kindle and Paperback

The Order for Morality and Justice has grown its power base and now reaches to the highest level of government. Virtually all civil rights laws are gone. The federal government is on the verge of declaring martial law nationwide.

Warrants are issued daily for the arrest of enemies of the state. When they come for Erin Foster and her partner of seven years, Alice, the Peacekeeper of The Order for Morality and Justice shoots out the front door lock. His bullet ricochets and kills Alice.

Alice's death flips a switch in Erin Foster and her mission to destroy The Order and its leader, The Reverend James Calton III, begins. In her eyes, you're either part of the solution or you're part of the problem.

Life Is Full of Surprises

What do industrial espionage, an unsolved hit and run and a bloody knife in an ice cream carton have in common? They're all elements in the romantic mystery Life Is Full of Surprises.

Barbara Orlock and Judy Langdon have both sworn off falling in love. They agree their relationship will be no strings attached, just fun and games.

Judy's ex-lover, Carol Engram, is found dead in Judy's apartment. Actin on an anonymous tip police search Barbara's freezer and find the murder weapon, a bloody knife, hidden in an ice cream carton.

Will Barbara's faith in her business associate, Gerald, be her undoing? Was the death of Barbara's previous lover, Linda, really an accident? Who has the most to gain by Carol's death? Or maybe the question should be who has the most to gain if Barbara is convicted of Carol's murder? Can Judy unravel the mystery and clear Barbara of murder?

The Origin of Deanna Dorak
Nedamla Book #1

Is she merely a freak of nature…or is she from another world?

Deanna Dorak suddenly finds herself alone in the world and begins to realize that it may not even be her world. With confusing images forcing their way into her consciousness she struggles to understand who she is and why she's here. She elicits the help of her best friend and former lover, Kate, who believes that all of Deanna's problems stem from her inability to accept her mother's death. That is until she sees the gills that have begun to form on Deanna's sides. Kate brings Deanna to Dr. Jason Alexander, who vows to help her and protect her from government scientists.

Soon after, Kate's body is pulled from the river – someone broke her neck.

A frantic search for answers takes Deanna on the quest of her life. Is she the reason her friend was killed? Is Jason friend or foe? Is he holding her captive for his own scientific research? Is she really from another planet, an underwater world inhabited only by women? Can she trust the detective assigned to solve Kate's murder? Can she trust herself?

Aneesha's Prophecy
Nedamla Book #2

"The daughter will return and avenge the death of her mother and those innocents killed here today."

Dorak Deanna has come home to claim her birthright. Home, to a planet she remembers only through the implanted memories of her mother, Miktra. Home to a planet still occupied by the same Empyrean forces that forced her departure nearly thirty years ago.

The Day of Ascension is fast approaching and the Empyrean Governor of Nedamla grows more fearful of Aneesha's Prophecy with each passing day. Especially since each day seems to bring another unexplained, violent death of at least one of his soldiers. Yet the Empyror refuses his requests for more troops, assuring him that since Aneesha's child was killed during the invasion, there is no heir to ascend to the throne.

By accident Deanna discovers she has the ability to communicate, with at least one Nedamlan, by using only her thoughts. Is it possible that there are others among her people with this ability? Perhaps it will be the secret weapon she needs.

Even with the ability to mind-talk, how can one woman turn a population of women, known for their pacifism, into warriors? And if she and her warriors take Nedamla from the troops now occupying her, how will they maintain their freedom? The Empyror has more than enough troops to simply send another invasion force.

As if fighting the Empyre weren't enough to worry about, Deanna has another problem – she has fallen in love.

Will Deanna fulfill Aneesha's Prophecy? Can she return her people to a time when they were fierce warriors, asking no quarter and giving none? Will Jorsta agree to join with her?

Made in the USA
Columbia, SC
11 October 2022

68629436R00119